I0589889

CYNTHIA HICKEY

Advance Notice

A River Valley Mystery

Cynthia Hickey

Copyright © 2014 Cynthia Hickey
All rights reserved.

No part of this publication may be reproduced or transmitted in any form or by any means without written permission of the AUTHOR.

All scripture quotations are taken from the Holy Bible, New International Version®. niv®. Copyright © 1973, 1978, 1984 by International Bible Society. Used by permission of Zondervan. All rights reserved.

This book is a work of fiction. Names, characters, places, and incidents are either products of the author's imagination or used fictitiously.

Any similarity to actual people, organizations, and/or events is purely coincidental.

ISBN-13: 978-1-0880-2746-2

DEDICATION

This book is for all my fans
who eagerly awaited the sequel to
Deadly Neighbors,
to my husband for his unfailing support,
To God for the never ending cornucopia of
ideas

1

"I am clearly not dead, Marsha Calloway. I'm standing right here." Mrs. Nina Worth shook a newspaper in my face. "But the obits clearly state I died two days ago from suspicious circumstances."

Where was Duane with my car? I stood on tiptoe, trying in vain to stretch my five-foot-two-inch body enabling me to see over the people milling in the church parking lot. "What would you have me do, Mrs. Worth? Why don't you call the newspaper and explain the mistake?"

"I want you to stop me from dying!" She wagged the paper closer to my nose. "Suspicious circumstances, Martha. That's ominous. And don't forget that poor Mae died three months ago, *after* seeing her name in the obits."

"That was ruled an accident." Oh, where was Duane? "Her stove exploded."

"Coincidence, I think not." Nina took a deep breath, her hands shaking. "When I wind up dead, you'll have no one but yourself to blame, girlie!" She stalked off in pumps the color of Big Bird from

Sesame Street. One of the bird's feathers fluttered from the silly over-sized hat she wore.

I shuddered at the eerie warning the floating feather seemed to give. The feather landed in a puddle and sank.

Nina over-reacted. There was no other explanation. Besides, why would she think I could do anything? Just because I solved a crime spree six months ago, did not make me a detective. Duane would kill me if I got involved in another mystery. He'd probably call off our wedding, if I had a date planned.

Why I hadn't decided on a date was beyond me. I loved the man with everything in me. You'd think I'd rush to be his wife. I sat on a concrete bench to ponder the reason while I waited for Duane. If he got stuck talking football, and since he was the high school football coach, it was a distinct possibility, I could be waiting for quite a while.

I dug my phone out of my purse and texted him. *Where are you?*

Mom, my daughter, Lindsey, and Mom's new husband, Leroy, all waved and climbed into Mom's giant white Cadillac. On their way to Wanda's Diner, no doubt. My stomach rumbled. Maybe I should have them come back and get me. Duane could meet us there.

Just as I was ready to call for them to return, Duane pulled up in my sky-blue Prius. I loved that car. Especially after what I'd endured getting it. Nothing like murder to make a purchase sweeter.

"Let's go to Wanda's," I suggested, sliding into the passenger side. "I'm pretty sure the rest of my family is headed there."

He leaned over to give me a kiss. "Sorry, I'm late. The pastor cornered me, and we argued about the Dallas Cowboy's merits. Of which I told him they had none." He grinned.

"Of course you did." My Pittsburgh Steeler loving boyfriend would do no less. "Nina Worth thinks she's dying because some prankster put her name in the obituary column of the newspaper."

"Why'd she hunt you down?" He drove the car from the parking lot and onto the highway.

"I'm guessing she wants me to find out why."

He cut me a sideways glance. "No more mysteries, Marsha. I'm serious."

"I won't." I chewed my pinkie nail. "But doesn't it strike you as strange? Especially after Mae Campbell's death?"

"She had a gas leak." His tone told me the discussion was over. "Leave it to the police."

I sighed and stared out the window until we pulled up at the Diner. As I'd suspected, my family was there. Mom's caddy took up two parking spots.

Duane and I exited the car and walked inside the diner, his hand warm on the small of my back. I'd never get tired of his touch. He still gave me goose bumps and sent my heart into overdrive.

"We knew you two would show up." Mom motioned for us to sit in the two empty chairs at the table. "This is becoming a regular Sunday event. Wanda must be so pleased."

"The place is busy, that's for sure." I stepped aside while Duane pulled out my chair. "Y'all must have called ahead."

"I did," Leroy said.

"What did Nina want?" Mom hooked her purse on the back of her chair. "She looked upset."

"Her name is in the obituaries." I blew a kiss at Lindsey, grateful for any time my teenager would spend in my company.

"Like Mae's?" Mom's eyes widened. "That's a bad omen, Marsha. You know it is."

Duane sighed and reached for a menu. "Here we go."

"Oh, stop." I slapped his shoulder. "I told her to call the paper and explain the mistake. Obviously, she isn't dead, and she looked healthy enough to me."

"Another mystery to solve sounds like fun." Mom folded her arms on the table.

"No!" Duane and Leroy yelled in unison, attracting the attention of everyone within hearing distance.

"Hush." Mom frowned. "You're making a scene. What if something happens to Nina? It'll be our fault for not taking her seriously. I always thought something was fishy about Mae's gas leak. That townhouse of hers was only ten years old."

"Gas leaks can happen anytime," Duane explained. "I don't want Marsha involved."

Mom and I exchanged exasperated looks. Men. "It won't hurt to make a phone call," I insisted. "Just one tiny call to the newspaper."

"Or one call a day to check on Nina." Mom pointed her finger at him. "Folks like to know people care. She's an old woman who doesn't have anything outside of church and that quilting club she belongs to."

"Quilting club?" First I'd heard of it. "Do they buy their supplies from us?" Most crafters around River Valley spent their craft dollars at Gifts from Country Heaven. Mom made me her official partner two months ago, giving me a sense of pride in the store. Owner sounded much better than employee.

"Yes, Marsha. No need for you to hound them. They meet there once a month to plan their projects, but they need a place to meet when they actually work on them, so they don't have to house hop. Leroy is going to build a back room onto the shop, and we can rent it out to crafters. Isn't that a great idea?"

"It is." I raised my eyebrows. Usually, Mom asked me for the new ideas. I shrugged. The newness of her newlywed status would wear off soon enough. No reason for me to feel as if my toes were getting stepped on. Besides, if Leroy wanted a part in the business, it made less work for me.

Duane grabbed my hand under the table and gave it a loving squeeze. As usual, he'd read my mind and felt the need to reassure me. I smiled, returned his squeeze, and turned to the waitress. "A bacon cheeseburger, no onions, and sweet potato fries. Oh, and a large Diet Coke. Thanks." I handed her the laminated menu and sat back while the others ordered.

Bruce Barnett, River Valley's very own Barney Fife, barged through the diner doors, his skinny chest puffed out like a Banty rooster. He scanned the room with a narrow-eyed gaze, then marched to a stool at the counter. The man always acted as if everything was an emergency.

I glanced out the window. He'd parked his squad car behind Mom's Cadillac. Here we go again. He'd take a leisurely lunch, making sure she waited a sufficient amount of time, as punishment for taking up two prime parking spots. Why didn't he give Mom a parking ticket and stop the silly feud?

"The nerve of that man!" Mom stood up fast enough to send her chair crashing into the person sitting behind her. "Sorry," she tossed over her shoulder before marching to the lunch counter. "Move your car this instant."

Bruce sipped his mug of coffee, acting as if he couldn't hear her, which he could. I'm sure folks in the next county could hear her. "Excuse me, Mrs. Bohan? Do you have a problem I can help with?"

"You heard me." Mom planted fists on her rounded hips. "You deliberately blocked my car."

"The same way you deliberately took up two parking spots." He carefully set his mug back in its saucer.

"That is to prevent dings in my paint job."

"Still not acceptable."

"Not against the law."

"It's rude."

Good grief. I stood and gave Mom 'the look'. "Get back over here before Wanda kicks us out." I turned to glare at Leroy. "Control your wife."

His bushy eyebrows almost disappeared under his hairline. "There's no controlling her, you know that. I've resigned myself to the fact it's only a matter of time before I have to bail her out of jail."

By this time, Mom and Bruce were standing nose-to-nose. They looked like two schoolyard kids having a staring contest.

"For crying out loud!" I stomped over and pulled Mom back to her seat. "Act your age. You're setting a bad example for your granddaughter."

"No, she isn't," Lindsey said, dipping a French fry into a glob of ketchup. "I think it's hilarious. All my friends love Grandma."

I hadn't noticed lunch being delivered while I refereed Mom and our Deputy Do-Right, but my stomach growled in appreciation as I sat down and hefted the quarter-pounder burger. I bit into beef perfection. A blob of ketchup plopped onto my chest. I sighed and grabbed a napkin. My natural food catchers never failed to do their job. Now, my favorite teal blouse had a stain.

"I can get that out." Mom waved a fork full of potato salad at me. "Oxy-Clean, that's the way to do laundry."

"Yes, I know." I kept my eye on her waving utensil, expecting a face full of her lunch at any moment.

Leroy must have seen the panic on my face, because he lowered Mom's arm and winked. "Yes,

Gertie, you're an undisputed wonder at doing laundry."

"And don't anyone forget it. I could teach lessons and make a good living, probably." She stared into space. "The next Queen of …Whatever. Laundry doesn't sound quite right, does it?"

The bell over the diner's front door jingled and Nina marched in and right over to Bruce. She tapped her foot, muttered something I couldn't hear, and stormed back out to the parking lot. I craned my neck to see what she'd do next.

She glanced right then left, and then proceeded to beat Bruce's squad car with her purse. I paused from eating, a sweet potato fry halfway to my mouth. By this time, everyone in the diner had their attention focused outside. Bruce cursed, grabbed his hat and dashed outside. He grabbed Nina's arm and attempted to pull her away from his car.

She kicked him in the shin with one of her yellow Big Bird shoes.

"Wow." I lunged to my feet and outside into the fray, dodging Duane's arm as it shot out to stop me. This was better entertainment than going to the movies.

"That's assault." Bruce rubbed his shin.

"Then arrest me." Nina hit him in the head.

I skidded to a halt. "What's going on?"

"I want to go to jail." Nina tilted her chin and crossed her arms. "This…this…baboon, refuses to arrest me." She raised her hand to strike again.

"Stop hitting me, you old bat!" Bruce unhooked his handcuffs from his belt. "You want to go to jail, fine. You're going to jail."

"Thank you, Jesus!" Nina grinned, showing a gap in her bottom teeth.

"Wait." I stepped up and took her arm, peering into her face. "Why do you want to go to jail?"

"Well, I figure they'll keep me for about thirty days for assaulting a police officer." She ducked her head as Bruce put her in the back of his car. "Once that thirty days is over, I'm safe. Mae died exactly thirty days after her obit appeared in the paper."

2

I pulled into the parking lot of the police station and cut the engine. Nina had managed to convince the judge to sentence her to exactly thirty days in jail. Now, here I was to give her a ride home. I figured the peace of the last month was about to be shattered.

Since she'd called me over thirty minutes ago, I'd expected her to be outside waiting. Yet, the autumn wind blew and there was no sign of Nina and her bright yellow clothes. I sighed and shoved open my car door.

"Yoo hoo!" Oh, there she was. Nina bounded down the steps. "Thank you so much for picking me up. Isn't it a glorious day?" She slid into the passenger seat.

"Yes, it is," I said, closing my door. "A bit chilly, though."

"Not compared to those jail cells. Do you know that they only let the inmates wear thin cotton shirts and pants? Kind of like what nurses wear, but not as nice of quality. And that pea green color. Oh, my."

Nina set her purse in her lap. "You know I'm partial to yellow. Bruce wouldn't even check to see if the uniforms came in yellow. He is a rude little man."

I listened to Nina continue to rant about the lack of proper food and the hard cot she'd slept on for the ten minutes it took for me to drive her home. I pulled onto the gravel drive leading to her house, then stopped in front of the garage. "Do you want me to come in and check things out for you?"

Her eyes widened. "No, that's probably not necessary. Although, I was wondering whether I should've had the judge hold me that one extra day. Today is the thirtieth day." She scrunched her mouth to the side. "I'll be fine. Mae died on the twenty-ninth day and was found on the thirtieth day, I think. Although, I could be wrong. Now, I'm just being silly. You go on home."

"How about I call you later?" My head was spinning from her calculations. If today were the thirtieth day, wouldn't that mean she should've stayed in jail until tomorrow?

"That's sweet of you. Call me around eight." Nina exited my car, slammed the door, I hated that, then hurried to unlock her front door.

The explosion rocked my car and belted it with gravel. Nina flew backward as if attached to a rope and yanked. I screamed and ducked as far as the steering wheel would allow. Nina! I shoved open my door, crawled out, and raced toward the house. My ears rang. My legs wobbled, giving me a weird lurch as I ran.

Flames shot out the door, gobbling the wood porch stretched along the house. I suspected the use of an accelerant, but couldn't stop to investigate. I also needed to stop watching so many crime shows.

Nina lay under a magnolia tree as if she were taking an afternoon nap. I fell to my knees beside her, the ground damp on the knees of my jeans, and felt for a pulse in the side of her neck that wasn't horribly burned. Nothing. The concussion of the blast probably killed her instantly, thank the Lord. To be conscious while her skin charred would be pain unmentionable. By the time I got to my feet, sirens wailed in the distance.

I no longer believed the names in the obituary column to be a coincidence. Once again, something was rotten in River Valley. Now, for me to convince the authorities of which there were few. With budget cuts and a town that mostly slumbered with no crime, our police force consisted of one Bruce Barnett.

Bruce arrived a split second before the fire truck that roared to a stop in front of the burning house. He stared at me over his steering wheel. His shoulders slumped before he shook his head and exited the squad car. "I feel sorry for Duane," he said marching past me. "Trouble follows you."

"I had nothing to do with this." I jogged to keep up with him. "I brought Mrs. Worth home, she unlocked her door, and BAM! She's dead under the magnolia tree."

"And yet, here you are." He turned so fast, we bumped noses. "Go home, Marsha. I'll be by later to fill out the report."

"I already told you everything." Did he not listen when I talked? "Except for the fact that today is thirty days after the announcement in the obituaries. Same as Mae Campbell. It is no longer a coincidence."

"Stop looking for a mystery. All the homes in this part of the city are old and probably not built to code. Go home."

"But—"

"Now! And don't leave town. I have questions for you. A lot of them."

"Fine!" If he wasn't so dense, it might have occurred to him that it was strange for Nina's gas to be on when she'd been gone for a month. She didn't strike me as a woman who would be that careless. Also, he might have stopped to wonder why the house blew up when she unlocked the door. But, since he was being such an obnoxious jerk, I wouldn't say a thing about a possible trap. Let him figure it out for himself. "I'm leaving."

I marched back to my car, tried to ignore all the pings in my doors and hood, and peeled out of the driveway, scattering my own fair share of rocks. Bruce Barnett made me so angry! Not to mention the horrible fact I'd watched a woman die. Put those two facts together, and my hands shook so hard I was afraid of driving into the ditch.

Blinking back tears, I drove slower than I needed to and crowded the shoulder of the highway. Hopefully, there wouldn't be any poor animals for me to run over.

"Look out!" I wrenched the wheel in order not to hit a young man. With my eyes full of tears, I almost didn't see him. He dove into a ditch. I slammed on my brakes, shoved the car into park, then rushed to his side. "I'm so sorry."

"You should watch where you're going." He got to his feet and brushed off the knees of his ragged jeans. "Are you trying to kill somebody?" He fished in his pocket for a lighter, pulled a cigarette from somewhere inside his vinyl jacket, and lit up.

"No. I said I was sorry. My name is Marsha Steele. Can I give you a ride somewhere?" I didn't usually pick up strangers on the side of the road, but considering I'd almost made him road kill, it seemed the least I could do.

"Danny Vera." He stuck his cigarette in his mouth, then thrust out his hand.

"Oh, you've been staying with your grandparents for several years, right?" I took in the layered hair spiked around his face, the skinny jeans, and black sneakers. A good-looking young man who should have better things to do in the middle of the day than hike down a major highway.

He nodded. "Off and on. I'm going to college at Arkansas Tech next semester. Thanks for the offer of the ride, but I live half a mile from here and prefer to walk. Be careful with your driving, Mrs. Steele." He blew out a puff of smoke and continued on his way. "No one should die before their time."

A weird thing to say. Frowning, I watched him saunter down the highway, his cigarette smoke leaving a gray haze over his head.

As I got in my car, my cell phone rang. Duane. "Hi, Babe."

"I just heard what happened. Are you okay?"

"I'm fine, just a little shook up." More than a little, judging by the way my hands still trembled. I glanced in the side mirror and pulled back onto the highway.

"Where are you? Do I need to come get you?"

"There's no need for you to leave work. I'm going home."

"I'll meet you at your mom's in ten minutes. Love you." Click.

Which was the same as going home, since I lived in Mom's guesthouse. I dropped the phone in my purse and pressed the gas pedal. The sooner I got home and into my bag of dark chocolate M&Ms, the sooner I'd start to settle down. The candy-coated chocolate made everything better.

My phone rang again, this time being my mother. News traveled fast in River Valley. "Hello, Mom."

"I heard what happened. Don't bother coming in to work today. I'll meet you at the house in ten minutes."

"Who's minding the store?" We couldn't all take off work because of an explosion.

"Leroy can handle it. I want to hear all the details." Click.

I sighed. I'd rather not relive them, especially with Bruce coming by later, but it appeared I'd have no choice. I'd have to tell the horrible afternoon's events over and over.

Thankfully, no news vans waited in the driveway when I got home. I hated that whole 'no comment' thing. The reporters didn't pay attention anyway. They made something up. Why couldn't the vultures leave folks alone and go straight to the police department for their information?

Ooops. I spoke too soon. The local channel news van sped up the road. I cut the ignition, grabbed my purse, and sprinted like an Olympic Champion for Mom's back door. Not only did I not like talking to the press, but I'd heard one of my high school non-buddies was now the main reporter. Stacy Tate was definitely not on the list of people I wanted to talk to. Especially after trying to steal Duane away during our Junior year of high school. Nope. I burst into the house. Not in the mood for her.

Dropping my purse on the counter, I opened the cabinet above the refrigerator, climbed on the counter, and grabbed my candy. Obviously, putting it out of easy arm's reach didn't work at keeping me from them, but it made me work a little harder when stress called, and I didn't feel quite so bad at ruining my diet.

"Marsha."

I whirled and screamed, almost falling from my perch. "Duane! You scared ten years off me."

"Sorry." He scooped me in his arms and marched to the living room, where he plopped both of us on the sofa, me on his lap. I clutched my purple bag and burrowed my face in his neck.

His arms tightened around me. "You're going to be the death of me, Marsha Calloway Steele."

"You've said that a hundred times, yet you still live." *Thank you, God.* I couldn't do without my bear of a man.

"Ready to talk about it?"

"No. Mom's on her way, too, then Bruce. I'd rather not go over it too many times. It was awful." I sniffed and tossed in a handful of therapeutic chocolate. "All I did was drive poor Nina home. I'm thinking she was right about the obit being a warning."

"Stop the wheels in your head right now." Duane tilted my face toward his. "You could've been killed today."

"Not really. I was in my car." The paint job was ruined. Maybe I wasn't meant to drive new vehicles. Something always happened to them. "Nina unlocked her door, and whoosh, fireball Worth flew across the yard."

"Marsha!" Mom fumbled getting her key in the front door. "Marsha! Why's the door locked? That evil Stacy is heading this way. Let me in."

"Should I?"

Duane shook his head. "No, this gives us a couple more seconds of privacy." He grinned. "Not enough of that with you living so close to Nosey Gertie."

I giggled and kept my head where it lay, watching the door bang open and Mom charge in. She rushed across the room and plopped next to us, taking my hands in hers. "First of all, you two should not be alone in the house without supervision, and—"

"Mother, I'm thirty-four years old."

"All the more reason. Secondly, tell me all about it. Oh, wait." She jumped to her feet. "Let me fix us some tea and grab some cookies." She flew to the kitchen.

"Let's make out before she returns," Duane suggested. "Get you all flustered and her imagination running wild."

"You're incorrigible." I lifted my face for his kiss and closed my eyes.

"But girls always fall for the bad boys." His lips covered mine, sending my heart into a race that even a thoroughbred couldn't win.

I slid my arms around his neck and pulled him closer, deepening my response. He smelled of a musky cologne and tasted of coffee. I wanted my fill before our chaperone returned.

The sound of footsteps alerted us to Mom's return, and I slid from Duane's lap, sitting as close to him as humanly possible without being on top of him. I rubbed my lips and blinked at my … daughter.

"Seriously? You have a fit if you see me kissing a boy, but it's okay for you to be all over Uncle Duane?" She took a deep breath. "Double standards. Oh, sometimes you make me so mad!"

"Is school out already?" I glanced at the clock.

"Don't change the subject." Lindsey tossed her backpack on the floor. "Did you know that Mariah's mom is having a baby? At her age? I don't want a baby brother or sister, Mom. Really!"

Duane and I glanced at each other and burst into laughter. We'd already said we'd try for a baby immediately after the wedding. I stopped laughing. Was that the reason I hadn't set a wedding date yet? Because I wasn't sure I wanted another baby?

3

"Why is Officer Barney sitting outside in his car?" Lindsey asked. "The last time he stopped by was because of a crime." She glared at me. "What did you do?"

"I didn't do anything." I unfolded myself from the sofa and moved to peer out the curtains. "I witnessed a crime today and Officer *Barnett*, not Barney, is here to take my statement."

"You are so embarrassing, Mom." She grabbed her backpack and stomped to the kitchen.

Me? How quickly she seemed to forget that the last crime we were involved in was because she was the prime person of interest. I sighed and let the curtains fall into place. "I might as well see what's taking him so long." I stepped on to the front porch and crossed my arms.

Bruce stared at me for a few seconds, then got out of his car. "Glad to see you're here."

"Where would I go? I live here. Were you sitting in your car trying to think of witty ways to irritate me?" Stacy, the well-dressed reporter, made a beeline toward us. "Hurry up before the vulture lands."

He increased his pace. "I'm here on police business, Marsha. You need to respect the badge."

"Whatever." I stepped aside and waved my arm for him to enter. Respect my right foot. This little weasel accused my daughter of theft not so long ago. He wasn't starting this newest misfortune off much better. I straightened my shoulders and marched back to the living room.

Mom entered with a tray of packaged lemon cookies and a pitcher of iced tea. She narrowed her eyes at Bruce. "You, again."

"Who else would there be, Mrs. Bohan?"

"I keep hoping they'll scrape the bottom of the pickle barrel for someone else." She set the tray on the coffee table and sat on the couch, leaving me room beside Duane.

Bruce glanced at all three of us. "I'd like to speak with the witness privately, please."

"Never mind." I shook my head. "I'm going to tell them anyway. Tea and cookies?"

"I'm on duty." He pulled a notepad from his pocket. "Please start at the beginning and tell me everything."

"Well," I dug into my candy, choosing one of each color. "A month ago on Sunday, Nina came to me and said—"

"What happened today?" Strain showed in his voice, and we'd just begun. Poor man.

"Okay, but that isn't the beginning." I peeled Duane's fingers off my leg where he squeezed in an attempt to get me to curb my tongue. "I picked Nina up from the jail and drove her home. She stuck her key in the lock of her house, and BAM!"

"And?" His pencil paused its scratching.

"That's it. You and the ambulance arrived shortly after. Great job on the quick response, by the way." I popped a blue M&M in my mouth and tried to ignore Duane's increasing pressure on my thigh. "I think she died on impact."

"This isn't much to go on." Bruce snapped the notepad against his hand. "Maybe we should go back to that Sunday. What happened?"

"Her name was in the obit column of the newspaper. She was still very much alive." I studied his face, noting his mustache now resembled Hitler's rather than the curved look of an old-fashioned cowboy like he usually wore. "She said the same thing happened to Mae Campbell. Obit, then death, instead of the other way around."

"Mrs. Campbell's death was from a gas leak."

"As Nina's appears to be until someone investigates further. Ouch, Duane, stop it." I slapped his gripping hand. "Way too similar of deaths, don't you think?"

Bruce stood. "I'll take it into consideration. Duane, keep her out of the investigation, please."

"I'll do my best." He fought, trying to keep me from pounding him, until he captured both my hands in one of his strong grips. What was wrong with everyone?

"Right. Well. I'll be leaving." He tossed a business card on the cookie tray. "Call me if you think of anything else."

Once he'd left, I yanked free of Duane and turned with the ferocity of a cornered cat. "What are you doing?"

"Trying to keep you from mouthing off and upsetting our local police department."

"I'll behave if he does. I'm going to have bruises on my knee, thank you very much." I rubbed the offending spot.

"I'm sorry, but I could tell you were working up a good steam of sarcasm." He kissed the tip of my nose. My legs went weak and whatever annoyance I felt from his death grip on my knee, went out the window. "Don't get involved, don't make people angry. Live to see another day. I love you. Now, I have football practice."

"Come for dinner?"

"Wouldn't miss it." He kissed me long and hard, unmindful of Mom's eagle eye. "I'll get rid of the news reporter for you."

I glanced outside. Sure enough, Stacy leaned against her van, microphone in hand, shapely legs crossed at the ankles. "Thank you. Don't let her try anything funny. I'll be watching from the window."

He laughed. "I wouldn't dream of it."

Way too soon, Duane stood next to the temptress in an expensively tailored red suit. She said something. He laughed. She giggled. My hands curled into fists. What would Stacy look like if I pulled out every strand of her honey-blond hair?

"Relax. Duane loves you too much for a vixen like that to take him away." Mom lifted the untouched tray. "Come on into the kitchen. I set the newspaper on the table before leaving for work this morning."

Would another living victim's name be in the obituaries? I prayed not, as I followed my mother. If we did find a name, how would we convince them to take care? So far, two victims had died of gas leaks in their house. If Nina's premonition had been taken seriously, would the killer have gotten to her somewhere else? If she had waited until tomorrow to go home, would the killer have found a way to get to her in jail? My head ached from more than the blast of the explosion.

I pulled the rubber band off the paper and spread the thin Wednesday edition out on the table. Only three names were listed, and I knew all three were deceased and from our church. I plopped into a chair and accepted the cup of sweet tea Mom handed me. "Mom, how long between Mae's death announcement and Nina's?"

"About thirty days."

"Exactly?"

"I didn't mark it on the calendar, Marsha. That would be gruesome." Mom opened the drawer by the refrigerator and pulled out a hot pink clipboard. "Until Nina mentioned it, I didn't think anything suspicious was going on."

I grinned, recognizing the notes I'd taken on our last mystery. "You kept it."

"Figured it would come in handy again." She handed me the board and a pencil. "Now, start writing things down."

"Duane will kill me."

"There's nothing against the law about taking notes." Mom sat across from me, clutching a sweating glass of tea. "What do the two victims have in common?"

Oh, but I did love the thrill of a good mystery. "They both went to our church." I wrote that down.

"And belonged to that quilting circle that will be meeting at our store soon." Mom pointed at the pad. "Add that. First chance I get, I'll head down to the newspaper office and see exactly when both obits were published. That will give us a better time line."

"Here." Lindsey entered through the back door, carrying my laptop. "I've been eavesdropping. The obits should be online."

"You're a genius." I turned on the computer and waited for the screen to boot up. "But it's wrong to listen in on other people's conversations."

"I know." She poured herself a glass of tea and joined us at the table. "But talking about murder is way more interesting than what you usually talk about."

Within minutes, we'd discovered that Mae's and Nina's obituaries ran sometime during the week thirty days before they died. I sat back in my chair. If the killer stayed true, there would be another obit sometime this week. I wrote down gas leak and put a question mark beside it. Was this the only way the killer offed his victims? Unfortunately, only time would tell. Sad that someone had to die in order for an MO to be brought to light.

I shut off the computer and sat it on the counter before hiding the notes back in a drawer. Duane would be back in less than an hour. I definitely didn't want him to know how I'd spent my afternoon. I'd plead curiosity, which would be the truth, but we both knew it probably wouldn't stop at that.

"Marsha, come fix the salad while I get the spaghetti water boiling." Mom handed me a large wooden bowl. "I'll make sure to pick up a paper tomorrow, and we'll go through it between customers at work."

"Don't forget, I have those placemats to finish." A customer had ordered two hundred white cotton placemats, complete with embroidered initials, for her wedding. "I still don't understand why you won't purchase an embroidery machine. It's taking me forever to finish."

"That's an expense we don't need, since God gave you two perfectly good hands."

"Hands that are quickly developing carpel-tunnel syndrome." I ripped into a head of iceberg lettuce.

"See," Lindsey said, setting her glass in the sink. "These are the types of conversations that I am not interested in hearing. Call me when supper's done. I'll be in the cottage doing my homework."

"Teenagers."

"Mothers."

We grinned at each other, then she sailed out the back door. Thank you, God, for the gift of a good kid. One who unfortunately, enjoyed mysteries as much as I did. I grabbed a tomato and started slicing. Between me, Lindsey, and Mom, we'd managed to solve a crime a few months ago, and stayed alive while doing so. Just call us the Three Musketeers.

My cell phone rang. I wiped my hands on a dishtowel, ignored Mom's complaint about wiping tomato hands on her white towel, and then fished my phone from my purse. Lynn.

"Hey, Bestie."

"Is your life so boring that you have to regularly get involved in death?" Lynn sighed hard enough to vibrate the phone.

"I didn't do it on purpose." Was there anyone in River Valley who didn't know I was there when Nina died?

"You never do. I thank the good Lord you decided not to take the aide position at the high school. Heaven forbid you should drag death to the school." Lynn taught high school English.

"You're being kind of harsh."

"Honest."

"Evil."

"Watching out for you."

"Fine." I propped the phone on my shoulder, not an easy task since it was a slim smart phone, and started rinsing the mushrooms.

Mom butted me with her hip. "Tell her I said hello."

"Tell your Mom I heard her and hello back."

Mom waved a water dripping spoon at me. "Ask her if she wants to join us in this current mystery. It might be good to have a college educated woman helping us."

"Mom said…"

"Tell your mother there is no way on heaven or earth I want to get involved. Gracious, Marsha."

"Do y'all want to talk to each other? Because I'm getting a crick in my neck." I dropped the mushrooms into a colander, shook them, and carried the lot to the table to chop.

My gaze fell on the paper. Fingers tickled up my spine. What if my name got posted next?

Or Mom's?

4

The next morning, I eyed the unrolled newspaper on the store counter. The information it might contain ate at me. What I should have been doing was keeping an eagle eye on the two teenagers in the store, who most likely skipped school that morning. Instead, they ogled and played with a display of Swarovski crystal earrings Lindsey had made. My daughter had a talent for making jewelry, if these girls' oohs and aahs were any indication.

When a van of residents from our local retirement community arrived, I realized it would be a while before I could sit down with the paper. I sighed and plastered on a smile as ten gray-haired ladies pushed through the door. Once inside, they scattered to the four corners in pursuit of their own delights.

One of the teenagers, oh so casually, slipped a pair of earrings in her pocket. Right out in the open, like I was blind or something. I was more than capable of watching the girls and the older ladies, and resented the girl's unspoken view of my abilities. I sashayed from behind the counter and stood by the front door. Arms crossed, legs spread shoulder width apart, I glared. "Put them back."

"What?" Her eyes widened. "I wasn't going to steal them. Just keep them there until I finished shopping."

"Right." I pointed. That's why she headed for the door. "Back. Now."

Face red, the girl hung the earrings back on the rack.

"Y'all take anything else?"

They shook their heads.

"Now, leave. You're no longer welcome in this store. I will look you up in the yearbook so I have names to go with your faces." I put my customer service smile back in place. "Have a nice day."

One of them called me a name that rhymed with witch. The other just glared as if she wanted to stick a knife in my back. No worries. I had a teenage daughter and was quite familiar with evil looks. But, I would still be phoning the high school principal about their ditching.

Soon, a line formed at the counter as the retirement home van honked outside. The residents bought everything from potholders to a quilt. By the time they left, my smile was no longer forced. It had turned into a very productive morning.

With the morning quiet again, I picked up the basket of wedding placemats and sat in one of the rocking chairs we had for sale and got to work. In, out, in, out, the needle and silver embroidery thread flashed, and my mind wandered. I really wanted to open that newspaper, but if I did before Mom got back from her shopping trip to replenish our supplies, she'd kill me. Literally.

I glanced at the clock. She'd been gone for over two hours. Had she left me to mind the store all day again? Since her marriage, Mom seemed more content to stay home with her new husband than tend the shop. I snipped off the thread and grabbed another placemat. Not that I could blame her. Once Duane and I got married, I wouldn't want to leave home either.

Why hadn't I set a wedding date? I loved him without a doubt. Was it because I felt guilty marrying the brother of my late husband? Sure, Duane was my first love, but he'd deserted me to move on to bigger and better things, leaving his brother to pick up the pieces. Was I afraid he would do it again? I shook my head.

We'd both grown up in the ten years he'd been off to college. Duane loved me with the love of a man now, not a teenage boy. I glanced out the window at the sight of said man. Why wasn't he at work? And why was he strolling down the sidewalk with Stacy hanging on his arm? I leaped up, placemats falling back into the basket at my feet.

Duane and Stacy entered the coffee shop across the street. I admitted Duane was probably on his prep time at school, but why would he be spending time with the one person I disliked the most in River Valley? My heart sank. Suddenly, I needed coffee in the worst way.

After flipping the sign to closed, and a little clock to show I'd return in fifteen minutes, I locked the store door and dashed across the street. Before barging inside like a maniac, I took a moment to breathe deeply and pat my hair into place. As usual, curls escaped my ponytail holder and danced in the abundant joy of freedom.

I headed straight for the counter where I ordered the largest mocha iced coffee they had, and a slice of lemon pound cake. While I waited, I scanned the room. There they were; in a cozy little corner. By the time the barista handed me my order, my neck burned. Still, I could play things cool. I strolled their way, clamping my teeth around the straw.

"Duane. Stacy. What a surprise."

His face reddened, and he leaped to his feet to pull out a chair. "Stacy is doing an article on the football team. Care to join us?"

I gave Stacy a simpering smile. "Delegated to high school sports? I'm so sorry."

She rolled her eyes. "The newspaper is cutting back on employees, so we all have to cover extra. With all the ways available to get the news electronically, subscriptions are way down." Her blood red lips parted in a grin. "But, I don't mind. It gives me the opportunity to reconnect with Duane."

"How wonderful." I slipped my arm around his neck and gave him a kiss he wouldn't forget anytime soon. "See you for dinner, sweetheart." With a pat to his cheek that might have been a little too hard for a love tap, I marched out the door and back to the store, feeling every inch the jealous wench that I'd proven to be.

Resuming my seat in the rocker, coffee in one hand, cake in the other, I continued to stare out the window as tears pricked my eyes. What an idiot I was. Just a harmless interview in a public place. Was I really that insecure? I owed Duane a huge apology, and a time of repentance spent with God.

Mom breezed through the door, arms loaded with bags and packages. "Look at all the bargains. We can make so many new things for the store." She dropped her purchases on the counter and took a quick sweep of the store. "Productive morning?"

"How do you do that? Know with one glance what is bought?" I shoved the last of the cake in my mouth and went to help her unpack.

"Experience. Besides, if you put everything in its place, it's easy to spot when something is gone." She narrowed her eyes and studied my face. "What's wrong? Is there something in the paper?"

"I was waiting for you before looking." I piled several skeins of yarn on the counter, seeing an afghan in my future. "Duane is across the street with Stacy having coffee. He said she's interviewing him about the football team."

"Tell me you didn't go over there and make a fuss." Mom planted fists on her hips. "No man wants a jealous woman, Marsha. Either you trust him or you don't." Her eyes raked my body. "It wouldn't hurt for you to start dressing more feminine, either. Overalls are not becoming."

But they hide a lot of body imperfections. "I trust him, but I couldn't help myself. It's an illness." The next things out of the bag were several boxes of crystals in every color of the rainbow. Lindsey would be thrilled. "Now, her...I trust about an inch."

"You know what I always say. Life is too short for foolishness." Mom stuffed the empty bag in a container so they could be reused. "Now, let's look at that paper." She popped off the rubber band and tossed it into a desk caddy.

The bell over the door jangled, signaling the arrival of more customers. Mom greeted them with a smile and, when they expressed interest in some crafting books, she moseyed their way to help them decide on a purchase. I started to think we'd never get to read the obits.

Duane and Stacy headed back down the sidewalk, Duane casting a somber glance toward Gifts from Country Heaven. Oh, yeah. Apology.

I fished my cell phone from my purse under the counter and texted him that I was sorry. I watched through the window as he read his text, then gave a thumbs-up toward me. I knew he couldn't see me, but I waved anyway, my heart lighter.

Obviously, Thursday was the new senior citizen's day at the store. Customers drifted in and out all day. It wasn't until almost closing time that Mom and I were able to open the paper. We bypassed the news and went straight to the obituaries, scanning the list of two names.

"Do you recognize either of them?" I asked.

Mom nodded, her face pale under her makeup. "Dotty Baker."

"Dead or alive?"

"Very much alive. We just sold her a book on quilts." Mom raced out the front of the store, returning within ten minutes with a fuming Dotty in tow.

Dotty's pink-tinted hair quivered with rage, reminding me of cotton candy on the end of a paper cone. "Have you gone completely crazy, Gertie? You should never drag a woman away from her date, much less a senior discount dinner at Wanda's."

"You weren't there yet." Mom tapped the paper. "Read."

"So? It's obviously a mistake." Her brow furrowed.

"Don't you follow the news?" I asked. "Mae Campbell and Nina Worth both had their names in the obituaries before dying in a gas leak explosion at their house thirty days later."

"I don't have gas in my house," Dotty explained. "All of the retirement units are run by electricity. Now, Marsha, Gertie, I know the two of you fancy yourselves amateur sleuths, but this time you've gone too far. I have a perfectly fine gentleman waiting for me at the diner." She glanced at her watch. "Thanks to you, I'm late."

"You'll be permanently late if you're dead!" Gertie poked her in the chest with her forefinger. "Do you think we've put your name in there on purpose? You ungrateful old biddy."

What exactly was going on here? "Ladies—"

"I wouldn't put it past you, you man-stealing—" Dottie's hair shook harder.

"Excuse me?" Mom stepped forward until their noses almost touched. "You can't take something from someone that never belonged to them."

Hmmm. Had Mom stolen Dad from Dotty? I thought of Stacy and Duane. How history did tend to repeat itself.

"Mom, Mrs. Baker, now is not the time or the place to rehash old arguments." I folded the paper. "This needs to be taken seriously."

"I don't have time right now," Dotty said. "I've got a good thing going with my present boyfriend, and I don't intend to let Nancy Drew and Miss Marple ruin it." She took a deep breath and fumbled in her purse, bringing out a tube of lipstick the same shade of pink as her hair. "Now, if you'll excuse me, according to the two of you, I only have thirty days to bring this man to the altar."

"Sarcasm doesn't become you, Dottie, dear." Mom tilted her chin. "Only the Lord suffers a fool."

"Leave me alone, Gertie. After dinner, I'm reporting you two to Officer Barnett. What an evil game you're playing just to get noticed in the River Valley News. Again." With those words, she flounced out of the store.

Mom and I glanced at each other, then shrugged. "We did what we could," Mom said. "She's never been the shiniest button in the jar."

"You know as well as I do, that she's going to be killed next." I rattled the paper. "We can't let that happen."

"I'll talk to her again, when she's calmed down." Mom smirked. "I probably didn't present things to her in the best way possible."

"What did you say?"

"Come with me if you want to live."

5

I mixed a salad for supper and kept glancing at the front door, waiting—hoping—for Duane to arrive. I'd taken his thumbs up as assurance he wasn't angry with me for my childish actions in the coffee shop. Maybe I'd interpreted the gesture wrong. Maybe it was only a sign that we would be talking, with me doing most of the listening. Sighing, I chopped through a red bell pepper until I had nothing but a diced pile on the chopping board.

"Foolish woman." Mom came inside from the back porch and slammed the phone handset on the receiver. "I tried again to explain to Dotty about her impending danger, but she hung up on me." Mom crossed her arms and glared at the phone. "Says we're making things up in order to get our names in the paper again. Stupid!"

"There's nothing we can do about it. We tried to tell her." If we were right, guilt would be almost overwhelming, despite knowing we'd done all we could. Especially, if something happened to the stubborn woman. There had to be a way to save Dotty before the month ran out.

I sensed Duane before I saw him. It amazed me how the air changed the moment he walked into a room. All my senses tingled. I whirled as he leaned against the kitchen doorframe, crooked smile on his face.

"I'm so sorry." Dropping the butcher knife onto the counter, I threw myself into his arms.

"You silly woman." He led me to a chair, then sat me on his lap. "There is no one but you. You hold my heart in your hands. Without you, my heart would never recover."

Sighing, I buried my face in the crook of his neck. A spot God had made just for me. "That woman has always made me behave like a crazy person."

"It's just an interview." His arms tightened around me. "I'm sure there will be more. You need to trust me, Marsha."

"I do. It's her I don't trust." My voice was muffled.

"So you've said." He chuckled and set me on my feet, then turned me to face him. His smile faded. "Now, to change the subject. Tell me you and Gertie aren't going to try and solve another mystery. Don't you remember what happened last time?"

"Yes, I remember, but if we don't do something, Dotty will die. I'm convinced of it."

He sighed. "I know you well enough to know you're going to do what you want, but I can still hope you'll be smart about it."

I bent and planted a kiss on his forehead. "I won't do anything stupid."

"Of course not." He gave me a playful swat on the rear. "Now get to cooking, woman. I'm starving. Sexy reporters who want to interview me always give me an appetite."

"Ha. I ought not to feed you after that remark."

"But you will."

"Yes, I will." I tapped his nose with my forefinger and stood. Straightening the bib on my overalls, I wondered whether Mom was right. Maybe I should wear a dress once in a while, or maybe a nice pair of capris. Then, I could set Duane's heart to fluttering the same way he did mine.

"What's the matter with you?" Mom asked as I strolled into the kitchen.

"I'm thinking of getting rid of the overalls." I opened the cabinet and pulled out five glasses.

Mom felt my forehead. "Are you sick?"

"Stop it." I set the glasses around the table. "Aren't you the one who's always saying I should dress more like a woman?"

"You never listen to anything I say. Get you some of those jeans with the sparkles on the butt." Mom pulled the steak from the broiler, set it on top of the stove, then marched to the back door. "Time to eat!"

Now all the neighbors knew. I shook my head and finished setting the table at the same time I heard Lindsey thunder across the porch. Leroy followed her, then Duane appeared from the living room. My family was complete.

Conversation ceased for the first few minutes of supper. Then, Leroy shattered the peace. "So, what did you two women do at the shop today?"

"Uh." Mom glanced at me and stuck a bite of meat in her mouth.

"We were very busy." I grinned. "The retirement home sent over a van full of citizens to spend their hard-earned retirement checks in our store."

"That's great." He glanced around the kitchen. "I looked for the newspaper this morning, but couldn't find it. Did someone move it?"

Mom choked. She always was subtle.

I reached over and pounded on her back. "I didn't move it." Well, I didn't, really. It sat on the counter all day, right where Mom left it.

Duane studied me over the rim of his glass. "There's something you aren't telling us. Marsha. You're a horrible liar."

"I took the paper." Mom took a deep breath, then a gulp of milk. "We wanted to look at the obituaries. Sorry, Leroy. I didn't even think how you enjoy the paper with your morning coffee."

"I almost called the newspaper office to have them deliver another one," he said.

"So," Duane wiped his mouth with his napkin. "What's in the obits?"

"Dotty Baker." Mom leaned forward. "Her name is in the obits, and she's very much alive and angry with me."

Mom had a tendency to run off at the mouth like a tsunami when cornered. I closed my eyes and let her go.

"Why, the very moment we saw her name, I tracked her down. She'd just bought some things from us. I warned her, but instead of being alarmed, do you know what she did?" Without waiting for a response, she continued. "She got angry with me for making her late for a date. Imagine that."

"Imagine that." Duane tossed his napkin on his plate and stood. "Marsha, may I speak with you outside, please?"

Uh-oh. I expelled a deep breath and nodded. Lindsey chose that moment to start clearing off the table and avoided my gaze. I stood and followed Duane's ramrod-straight back to the yard.

He continued to the back fence, then gripped the top rail. "You're going to get involved."

"How can I not? Bruce doesn't believe there's anything to be concerned about." I stood with my back against the wood rail and stared into his stony face. "I can't stand back and let another woman die."

"I'll talk to Bruce. Convince him to call in backup. Even he has to consider the fact now that two women have died." He glanced at me.

"What if Mom's name turns up in the paper?" I kicked at a dead leaf near my foot. "Or mine?"

His shoulders slumped. "I almost lost you, Marsha. That crazy woman did poison you."

"And you."

"We're not talking about me!" Raking his hands through his hair, he shook his head. "I couldn't live if something happened to you. Why can't you stay out of these things?"

Why couldn't I? Was it the thrill of outsmarting a killer? Of rubbing into Bruce's face that I could solve something he couldn't? Was I so desperate for better self-esteem that I had to put myself in harm's way in order to feel like somebody? I stared into Duane's eyes. They darkened in the gathering dusk: Eyes so full of pain and love that stabbed at my heart.

"I don't know," I whispered. "It's like the mystery cries out to me. I don't go looking for them, you know that. Yet, here I am, thrust into another one."

"Is that why you haven't set a wedding date?" He put his hands on my shoulders. "Because, as your husband, I would have the power to tell you no?"

Power? I frowned. "You can tell me no, now. I'll try to honor your wishes, but no man will ever have power over me, Duane. Your brother tried, and failed." That was it.

The reason I balked at setting a date. I was afraid one Steele brother was the same as the other. It had crushed me when Duane ran off after graduating "to find himself". While my first husband, Robert, loved me, of that I had no doubt, he'd never let go of the fact that I'd loved his brother first. To compensate, he'd tried to rule over me.

"I love you, Marsha, but I can't talk about this right now." He whirled and stormed around the corner of the house, leaving me as alone as Robert had at his death.

Tears welled in my eyes and ran down my cheeks. Not able to face the rest of my family, I turned and entered the guesthouse. The two-bedroom, cottage-style house had always been a sanctuary to me, even before I'd cleaned and renovated it. Now, looking around at the comfy furnishings, they brought me no pleasure.

Had I run Duane off for good this time? Would he smarten up and break off our engagement? I plopped on the sofa and hugged a pillow to my aching chest. I'd tell him right now that I wouldn't work on the mystery. I'd beg him to forgive me.

After digging my cell phone out of the bib pocket of my overalls, I punched in his number. "I'm sorry," I said before he could say a word. "I won't work on this mystery. Go to Bruce, tell him our concerns. Don't be mad at me. Don't…break up with me."

"Sweetheart." A shadow filled my doorway, and there he stood.

With a sob, I threw myself into his arms. "Forgive me for being so stupid?"

He gathered my face in his hands and kissed me. "Always. I'll respect your wishes, Marsha, but you have to respect mine, too. If you want to dabble in another mystery, can you at least promise me that you'll let me know where you are at all times? That you'll tell me when you go somewhere and when you return? I'll be out of my mind with worry." He leaned his forehead against mine.

"I can promise that, Duane. Easily." I laid my face on his chest. "And I won't do anything unless

Bruce refuses to listen to you. And I won't go anywhere without Mom."

He chuckled. "I'm not sure you being with Gertie is much of a relief, but I'll take what I can get."

"I think all the victims have been a part of that quilting group that will be meeting at our store." I tightened my hold around his waist. "I can ask questions and never leave work."

"You have a one-track mind, Marsha Steele." He pulled free and laid his arm around my shoulder. "Your Mom made a chocolate cake for dessert. Interested?"

Grinning, I nodded. "You bet."

"Then come, my little gumshoe. You can't solve a mystery without chocolate fortification."

"I love you." The man made me so happy, I couldn't think straight. Knowing he believed me about the deaths, and was willing to talk Bruce into taking things seriously, warmed me better than any chocolate ever could.

Now, knowing that he supported me, I could call the newspaper tomorrow and find out exactly how someone can put an obit into the paper without checking out the facts.

6

"Yes, I'd like to find out how to put an obituary into the paper." My hand sweated around the phone receiver. Silly, really, since the conversation was over the phone.

"My condolences." A nasally voice on the other end sounded anything but compassionate. More like bored. "Our obits are done online and pulled from there before the paper is printed. Would you like the link?"

"No one verifies that the person really died?"

The woman paused. "Why? It isn't like people go around pulling pranks by putting someone's name in the obits while that person is still alive."

"Excuse me, but don't you read the paper you work for? That's exactly what is happening."

"Did someone put your name in the obits?"

"Well, no, but..."

A heavy sigh vibrated against my ear. "Is there anything else I can help you with? We're understaffed, and I have a lot of work to do. So, unless you want a job, I must let you go."

"No, thank you. That's all." I hung up and stared out the kitchen window, pleased that I'd discovered something about the case, but discouraged that I had no suspects. Online obituaries? Anyone could list anyone that way. I chewed the inside of my lip. How in the world were we supposed to find out who was behind the deaths of the three elderly ladies?

"Good morning." Mom bustled into the kitchen and headed straight for the coffeepot. "Lindsey gone already?"

"Yes, about fifteen minutes ago." My A-personality type daughter couldn't stand being late for anything, even school. "Mom, did you know all you have to do to get an obit in the paper is to fill out a form online?"

She turned from the coffeepot. "That makes everything a bit too easy, doesn't it?"

"Too easy." I got up and fetched my notebook from the drawer beside the refrigerator. Written in red ink across the top page was "Be Careful". That Duane. He was something else. With a smile on my face, I grabbed an ink pen and sat back down. "Okay. What do the three victims have in common other than being members of the quilting club?"

"They were all elderly. At least sixty." Mom poured us both a cup of coffee and brought them to the table. "And, they lived alone."

Who in the world would have a grudge against a bunch of elderly quilters? "How much longer until we can start hosting that group in our shop?"

"Immediately, if we give up the back room until Leroy's done building the addition. Why?"

"Because those silver-haired ladies are our only suspects." I supposed we could give up the room. We laughingly called it the break room, but when you owned your own business, breaks were few and far between. When I did have the pleasure of a down moment, I usually headed across the street to the coffee shop.

"Right." Mom nodded, her lips set in a thin line. "I'll call the leader, Betty Larson, the minute we get to work. She'll be pleased."

"I think I'll visit the newspaper. See what's really going on down there. Have you heard the paper is in trouble?"

She shook her head. "No, but it doesn't surprise me. That Frank Powell is a sour-faced man with a personality to match."

While Mom headed to Country Gifts from Heaven, I perused my scanty wardrobe. Since I'd chosen to stop wearing my overalls, except for yard work, I badly needed to go shopping. Nothing in my closet seemed fit to wear to the newspaper office. I pulled out an ankle-length dress from two decades ago and tossed it on the bed, then knelt to dig through my collection of flip-flops, finally choosing an orange pair that matched the flowers in the dress's fabric. Oh, who was I kidding? That dress would age me by thirty years.

I fell onto the bed alongside the outdated clothes. Capris and blouse it would have to be, no matter how chilly the autumn day. If I wore them to church, they should be all right for a small town newspaper. Maybe if I put a cardigan over the blouse, it would look more businesslike. Wasn't layering in style?

By the time I was dressed and slapped on a touch of makeup, Mom had already had the store open for an hour. She'd have my hide when I finally showed up. Grabbing my car keys off a small table by the front door, I dashed outside and tried to ignore all the dings in my car's hood. Maybe I could get Duane to call the insurance company for me. I tended to cave when faced with conflict. What if they didn't want to cover damage by murder?

Fifteen minutes later, I parked in front of the small red brick building that housed the River Valley News. Only two other cars sat out front, telling me that business was indeed slow for the local paper.

I took a deep breath and entered the building. A frazzled woman, pencil stuck behind her ear, answered the phone with the same nasally tone I'd heard earlier. She rolled her office chair back and forth between the phone and her computer. Somebody ought to bottle the woman's energy. I never would have known from the flighty way she moved around, that this woman was the same one with so little emotion in her voice.

"Excuse me." I stepped up to the Formica counter.

"Hold on." She twirled in my direction. "Yeah?"

"I'd like to see Frank Powell, please." I shoved my hands into my pockets, then realizing the action probably strained the fabric of my pants across my plump rear end, removed them.

"Do you have an appointment?" She typed something on her keyboard.

"No, but I—"

"Doesn't matter." She waved a red-taloned hand in the air. "He ain't busy anyway. Nobody works around here but me."

I wandered in the general direction of her hand, down a hall, stopping in front of a door with clouded glass and a nameplate stating Frank Powell. I knocked, and entered when commanded to. A thick smog of cigarette smoke explained the clouded glass.

Frank Powell, a short man whose stomach strained the buttons of his faded yellow shirt, tried in vain to wave the smoke out an open window. "Right with you."

I held my breath and waited.

"Here for a job? Which one?" Mr. Powell rifled through a stack of papers on his desk. "I've five."

"But, I—"

"You look perfect for our woman's advice column. No? How about local gossip? Advertising? Well, speak up! I haven't all day."

"I, well…" What in the world? Since when was I ever at a loss for words? "Local gossip?" Oh, Mom was going to kill me! "Is it an anonymous post?"

He narrowed his eyes. "Of course. What bozo wants to write about other people's dirty laundry and then have them know who they are? That's suicide. You can work from home. Pay is five hundred a month, take it or leave it, and you have to come in for two hours once a week. You submit your column to me online, then come in on Friday mornings for me to tell you whether I like it or not.

"And while you're out gallivanting around, see if you can scare up any advertising. Here's the price list. You get fifteen percent of every ad you sell." He leaned back in his chair and crossed his arms. "There. I managed to palm off two jobs." He grinned, revealing tobacco-stained teeth, and rubbed his hands together.

Guess I now had another job. Oh, well. I could use the money for wedding expenses. First ad I'd sell would be from Country Gifts. I thrust my hand out for a shake. "It's a deal."

"Give the woman at the front desk your information. She'll take it from there."

Dismissed, I headed back out to Miss Personality. "I've just been hired."

"Oh, goody for you." She pulled several sheets of paper from a drawer. "Fill these out and return them to me ASAP. If you want to get paid, that is."

"I'm Marsha Steele." I held out my hand again.

She stared at it for a moment before returning my handshake. "Darla Quincy, Jill of all trades."

"Have you been here long?" I thought I knew everyone in River Valley, but I'd never seen her before.

"About a month. Frank hired me on the spot, much to my demise, but a gal's got to work." She narrowed her eyes into a piercing stare.

I could take a hint. I moved to a round table and got to work filling out the employment forms. When was I going to have time to write a gossip column? I'd barely passed high school English. Maybe Lindsey could help.

By the time I finished filling out the forms, my stomach rumbled, reminding me I hadn't eaten breakfast. With a bounce in my step, I handed the papers to Darla.

She raised penciled on eyebrows. "Let's see how chipper you are after a few weeks."

"I've never had a job before, other than working for my mother. This is exciting." I still didn't know how I would accomplish everything, but somehow, with God's help, I'd manage.

"Frank must be desperate." She tossed the papers in a wire basket on her desk. "See you Friday morning."

I refused to let her bad nature spoil my good mood. Mom would do that once I got to work. Instead, I drove to the alley behind the shop, parked, then snuck around the corner so Mom wouldn't see me going into the coffee shop.

Focused on the barista, who smiled a greeting, I almost missed Duane and Stacy cozied up in the corner. "The usual," I called to the barista before making my way over to my fiancé and the woman out to snatch him with her ruby red claws.

"More interviews?" I bent and gave Duane a lingering kiss. One glance out the side of my eye at Stacy's peacock blue suit, and I vowed to go shopping for clothes after work.

"Should be our last one," Duane reassured me. "Join us? I have another ten minutes before I head back to the school."

"I'm not sure if it will be the last interview." Stacy gave me a simpering smile. "I want this article on the football team to be front page. I'm sure I'll have more questions."

"I'm sure you will." I waved for my drink and pulled out a seat. Being a regular customer, the barista wouldn't mind too much that I asked her to deliver my drink. I also didn't intend for Stacy to have any time alone with Duane than was absolutely necessary.

"Seems we'll be working together off and on." I chose not to tell her I was the new gossip columnist. That was supposed to be a secret, right? "I'm gathering advertising for the newspaper."

"Really?" Stacy shrugged one thin shoulder. "Well, not exactly the same as reporting news, but it's a start."

"Just some pocket money to help pay for the wedding." There. Top that, you man-stealer.

"But, I thought—"

I kicked Duane under the table, keeping a smile on my face, to stop him from blurting out that we'd agreed to stay inexpensive and split the costs. Regardless of what we'd discussed, I now discovered I wanted a wedding dress that would wow the guests. I grabbed my coffee with my ring hand, making sure the diamonds faced Stacy. "We're going to have a wedding like no one has ever seen in River Valley." Which considering it was me getting married was most likely very true. I was known to stray off the beaten path.

Now, all I needed to do was set a date.

7

"You're late." Mom slammed the cash register drawer. "The shop has been extremely busy, and the customer with the placemats called to see how long until they're finished. Her wedding is less than a month away."

"I got a job." I slurped my coffee. "The placemats should be finished by the end of the day."

"Yes, that's my point. You have a job. Every time you get involved in a mystery, your work suffers." Mom shook her head and tossed me one of the ruffled aprons we'd chosen as our uniform. "What's wrong with you?"

I set my drink on the counter and donned the apron. What had her knickers in a wad? Mom was always just as thrilled to have a new puzzle to solve as I was. "I mean, I have a real job. I now get advertising for the paper, and," I leaned closer to her. "Gather local gossip for a column."

"When on God's green earth are you supposed to find time to do all that? Sometimes, I wonder if God gave you the sense He gave a goose. And that ain't saying much." She shoved the basket of placemats into my hands.

"The quilting circle will give me plenty of fodder for my column." Seriously, couldn't she give me a little credit? "I went in there to see if I could find out something about the obit column and ended up having a job thrown at me."

"Learn to say no."

"I found I didn't want to." Concentrating on threading the needle spared me from seeing my mother's irritated gaze. But I caught the vibe out of the corner of my eye. "This is the first job I've ever had, other than working here. Before Robert died, I stayed home and cared for Lindsey."

"But how will you have time?" The hurt in Mom's voice caused me to lift my head.

"Are you afraid I'll leave you? Mom, I'm getting married again." Someday. "No one knows whether I'll stay in River Valley forever." Very true, since Duane saw fit to leave town once before. Except this time, should he choose to leave, I'd be able to go with him.

"This is our business, Marsha." Mom sniffed and wiped her eyes on the hem of her apron. "Someday, it'll be yours and Lindsey's."

"It's a part-time job taken on the spur of the moment to help prevent Dottie from becoming another victim." I set the mats in their basket and went to put my arms around Mom. "It's something that will only take a couple of hours a week. Besides, who's better at gathering gossip than you?" I grinned. "You can tell me what to write."

"You made Cs in English." Mom gave me a wobbly smile. "I might as well write the column, too."

"Whatever makes you happy." After giving her another squeeze, I returned to work. "Did you contact Betty Larson?"

"Yes, they want to start on Thursday."

Day after tomorrow? That didn't give us much time. "How are we supposed to get the room ready?"

"Leroy hired some young man to help him. They'll clear the old room for us before starting on the new one."

Hammering outside the back door alerted me to the fact the men had already started. Mom was very convincing, when she wanted something done. It didn't hurt that Leroy was still in the throes of honeymoon bliss and retired. He had all the time in the world to succumb to Mom's wishes. I opened the back door and almost ran over Danny Vera.

The young man frowned and whipped his head, slinging his long hair out of his eyes. "You like running over people, don't you?"

"You two know each other?" Leroy glanced up from where he hammered a two-by-four onto another slab of wood.

"Briefly." I smiled at Danny, trying unsuccessfully to melt the scowl on his face. "I almost hit him with my car a couple of days ago."

Leroy shook his head and mumbled something about women drivers. That elicited a flicker of a smile from Danny. "This young man is skilled with a hammer and has some knowledge of electrical wiring. You leave him be."

"Yes, sir." I stepped back into the shop and closed the door. Men. They sure had their boundaries as to where women belonged when heavy work was going on.

Picking back up the embroidery, I settled into the rocking chair and let my mind wander. Three elderly ladies, two dead, one threatened. Obits in the paper before their death, which turned out to be a relatively easy thing to accomplish. The two deceased women died from a gas explosion. I sighed. I had nothing. No other clues and no suspects. I let the placemat fall to my lap.

Time was ticking, and Dottie Baker's days were numbered. I knew it in my gut, and I had no idea how to save her. The thought that the next name listed might be Mom's, chilled my blood. But the other women had lived alone, with no family. Was that the key to the mystery?

The bell over the door jingled. I pulled my mind from my musing to watch Duane stroll in. One look at the clock showed he was on his short lunch break. I set my work in the basket at my feet and stood to greet him with a kiss.

"Hey, good looking." He returned my kiss and added a hug. "Now, tell me about this job of yours, and why I shouldn't be as nervous as a raccoon surrounded by hunting dogs."

"It's just part-time. I'm selling advertising space for the paper and collecting gossip for the gossip column, but that part is a secret." I motioned for him to sit in one of the rockers we had for sale.

"I went in to snoop about the obituaries and walked out with the job. It was a total surprise."

"And?"

"There's no reason to worry. Both jobs are perfectly safe."

"Not snooping into other people's business." A frown line appeared between his eyes, and I clenched my hands to keep from smoothing it away.

"Don't be silly. The quilting club starts on Thursday. All I have to do is eavesdrop, or ask Mom for details. I won't have to leave the shop to gather enough gossip for ten papers."

"I hope not. I agreed to let you snoop…safely." He leaned over and kissed me again before standing. "I love you, Nancy Drew. Now, I've got to get back to work. Dinner?"

"In or out?"

"How about I take you out for steak? I'll pick you up at five thirty."

"Perfect." I picked up the embroidery and set to work on the last one as my handsome hunk of a man strolled back out the door, leaving me happy and peaceful.

"Maybe I'll get Leroy to take me out to dinner, too," Mom said, coming from the back room with an armful of quilts.

"I was kind of hoping you'd watch Lindsey." I cut the last stitch of thread. "Done. You can call the happy bride now."

"Your daughter is almost sixteen. Perfectly old enough to stay home alone for a couple of hours." Mom placed the folded quilts on a rack. "Since we need to clean out the back room for now, we might as well set out everything we have for sale." She planted her fists on her hips and surveyed the room. "Sure will make it crowded in here, though."

"How about placing an ad in the paper for an overstock sale?" I hefted the basket and slid it behind the counter.

"That's a thought. We've never done much advertising."

"What kind of stipulations did you put on the quilting club? Are you charging them for the room?" I grabbed a broom and started sweeping up bits of silver thread I'd dropped.

"They had to promise to buy all of their supplies from us." Mom dragged a big box from the store room. "Good thing I bought all these scraps of fabric at the discount store. Once we get them rolled and priced, we can set them out next to the quilting books."

A slow selling day, but by the time we finished cleaning out the "club" room, my feet and back ached. Mom was right. The front of the store looked crowded. Hopefully, Leroy and Danny wouldn't take too long to get the extra room built on. After that, there was no more room for expansion. Not unless we wanted part of the shop to be in the alley. Maybe Mom should look into moving to a larger property.

"Hi, Mom. Hi, Grandma." Lindsey waltzed through the door and tossed her backpack on the floor. "Who's the guy out back? He's kind of cute."

Danny? Never in my wildest dreams would I have classified that sullen young man as someone

Lindsey might be interested in. "He's too old for you."

"I didn't say I wanted to marry him. Good gravy!" Lindsey stomped through the back room, returning a moment later with a soda from the refrigerator we kept there. "Maybe I should take him a drink," she said, as if she'd never left the room. "It's kind of a hot day."

"I'm sure Leroy is taking care of him." I speared her with my mom look. "How's your photo shop class in school coming?"

"Good, why?" She narrowed her eyes at me over her Mountain Dew.

"We need a half-page ad for the paper saying we're having an overstock sale. Can you handle it?" Anything to keep her from making googlie eyes at a sullen young man.

"Easy." She cast another glance over her shoulder toward the alley. "Something simple or folksy?"

"Somewhere in the middle?" I suggested.

"With our logo." Mom waved a couple of knitting needles at her. "Don't forget that. We want folks to know who's having the sale."

Lindsey and I exchanged exasperated glances. "Of course, Grandma. I'm not stupid."

"Watch your mouth." I wiped the back of my hand across my sweating forehead. "Duane's taking me out to dinner tonight. Will you be all right on your own?"

She nodded. "I have homework and can work on the ad. How much are y'all going to pay me?"

I didn't raise a fool. "Fifty dollars?"

"Done." She finished her soda and retrieved her backpack. "I'll meet that guy some other time. Him and Leroy look all dirty and sweaty anyway. They probably stink." With those words, she sashayed out the door.

Maybe I needed to make sure Danny always looked stinky. Since Lindsey broke up with her previous boyfriend, Bobby, star of the football team, she'd been on the prowl for a newer model. I shook my head. Teenagers.

"Don't worry," Mom said. "She's a good kid."

"I know. I thank God for that every day." And I did. Not being exactly un-devious as a teen, I was thankful Lindsey seemed to have her head on straighter than I did. I'd drooled after Duane like a puppy after a bowl of water. Then, the moment he ran off after graduation, I'd upped and married his brother within six months. Nope. Not exactly level headed.

Dottie Baker barged through the front door. "Well, I'm still alive!" She made her way to the front counter.

"You have thirty days from when I warned you." Mom glared. "Are you here to buy something or to harass me?"

"I want to look at the jewelry your granddaughter makes. I've got another hot date tonight, and I want to look as young as possible."

I turned to hide my grin. With her pink hair, heavy makeup and deep wrinkles, Dottie would never look young again.

"Might as well live it up while you can." Mom waved toward the jewelry display. "Who's the unlucky man?"

"Dwight Linney." Dottie patted her hair. "He owns the feed store and is quite a catch."

"I know who he is." Mom shook her head. "The man's as old as medusa."

"And loaded." Dottie winked and pulled a butterfly bobby pin heavily studded with crystals from the display and slid it across the counter. "Twenty dollars is a bit steep, isn't it?"

"Nope, not for Swarovski." Mom rang her up and held out her hand. "Cash or credit?"

"Check." Dottie opened a purse the size of a satchel and dug around in its purple confines. "I don't want anyone knowing anything about me by stealing my identity."

"People won't need to steal your identity if you wind up dead." Mom's voice rose.

"If you don't stop threatening me, Gertie Bohan, I'll go straight to Officer Barnett! Then, if I do end up dead, you'll be the prime suspect." She grabbed her purchase. "Wouldn't that just suit you fine?"

8

By Thursday, my nerves were shot. The feud between Mom and Dottie had to stop. Why couldn't the old biddie see that Mom only wanted to help her? With only three weeks left before the deadline, my stomach churned. Especially knowing that Dottie would be one of the quilters meeting at the shop in an hour. I'd have the pleasure of listening to more back and forth insults from her and Mom.

I set a pitcher of iced sweet tea and a tray of Snickerdoodle cookies on a side table. Mom said it wouldn't do not to have separate snacks for the ladies. They wouldn't want the same ones we had in the main shop with the coffee. They needed to feel special.

Whatever. The bell over the door, followed by loud voices, announced the women's arrival. I squared my shoulders and prayed I could work the front of the store and let Mom flutter around the ladies. Of course, if I did that, I might not pick up any juicy gossip. I was in a quandary.

"Don't just stand there." Mom straightened the pile of napkins, then turned with a gracious smile. "Greet our guests."

"Good morning, ladies." I forced a smile. "The shop opens in thirty minutes, but I can help you now, if you need to purchase anything."

Mom stomped my foot. What? Weren't we here to make money?

Hammering started outside, competing with the women's conversation. Oh, this could get interesting. Maybe I would stay and let Mom run the store. Sure enough, not ten minutes in and before the first needle pierced the backing of the first square, Dottie and Betty glowered at each other, then at me.

"Do we have to listen to that the entire time?" Betty practically crumpled the square in her hand. "I'll have a frightful headache. We may have to reconsider our choice of meeting place."

"Just be glad they aren't trying to kill you," Dottie said. "I still say we should have checked to see if we could meet at the church."

"We are not trying to kill you." I opened the back door. "We're trying to keep you alive." Her strident voice as she explained the circumstances to the other women followed me.

"Leroy, the girls are complaining about the noise." I slowly closed the door so it wouldn't slam.

"You want this room finished or not?"

"It's going to be bad for business." I caught sight of Danny lurking around the corner. Most likely afraid I'd bump into him again. "Hey, Danny."

"I suppose we could spend the morning sawing. Or will that bother the queens?"

What was up with Leroy? My usually mild-mannered stepfather acted like he had a burr in the waistband of his underpants. "That should be fine. Thank you." Come to think of it, Mom was a little snippy, too. I had more than one mystery to solve.

I marched inside, took Mom by the hand, and dragged her out of ear shot of the other women. "What is wrong with you and Leroy? Are y'all having problems?"

"No." Her eyes widened, then filled with tears. "He wants me to sell you my half of the store so we can travel. That silly man wants to buy an RV."

Didn't sound like much of a problem to me. "So…you're upset because your husband wants to spend every waking moment with you. The nerve!" I tried to keep my mouth from twitching, and failed.

"It's not funny." She pulled a tissue from the pocket of her apron. "I love this store, but I love Leroy, too. What will we do with the house?"

I chewed my bottom lip, still not knowing what the problem was. "Lindsey and I can move into the house. I can hire part-time help here at the store, and you can be a silent partner. That way, if y'all get tired of gallivanting around the country, you can come back to work."

She cupped my face. "I raised the smartest daughter in River Valley, if not the entire world."

"Agreed." I gave her a hug then a gentle shove back to our guests. "Go find me some juicy gossip."

Part-time help wouldn't be difficult. Lindsey was my first choice, and I was sure one of her friends would be willing to earn some money. The long days might be harder to fill, especially with my two-hours a week of checking into the newspaper. But, if I'd learned anything in my life, it was that God worked everything out. All we had to do was trust and wait.

Danny slipped through the front door, his hair hanging in his face. "Leroy wants to know if there's any more tea, or if the women drank it all."

"I can make more. Tell him I'll be out in fifteen minutes."

The young man nodded and skedaddled as silently as he'd come in. That boy had a story for sure. Maybe one day, I'd have time to find out what it was.

By the time I had the tea made and delivered to the hard working men out back, the women had stopped stitching to take a break. At the rate they were drinking, I'd need another pitcher of tea for them, too. I turned toward the small kitchenette counter as the bell over the door announced a shopper. The quilters would have to wait.

Stacy stepped inside and stopped. Her perfectly made-up face crinkled, and I fought back the urge to tell her such a look would cause wrinkles that no amount of expensive makeup would cover. She heaved a dramatic sigh. "This place is so cutesy it makes me want to gag."

"Can I help you?" My frosty tone matched hers.

"Just point me to the quilters. Frank seems to think their new group is newsworthy." Shaking her head, she ran her hands down the skirt of her pinstriped gray suit. "I told him to let you handle the mundane type of articles, but he said you aren't ready."

"I don't do the news." Just gossip. I grinned, wondering whether there was some juicy tidbit I could post about her. "The ladies are through that door."

Chin tilted, shoulders squared, Stacy clutched a notebook to her chest and sashayed her way out of my sight. Her entrance seemed to open the floodgates, and I stayed busy with customers for the next half-hour. By the time the last one left, there was fifteen minutes left of the quilters' time. I hadn't had the opportunity to glean any gossip for my column. With one last glance at the empty door, I hurried into the back room.

"You are a mean, spiteful woman." Dottie pointed an arthritic finger at Stacy. "Just because you waltz in here with your fake...boobs...you think you're better than the rest of us. Well, let me tell you, girlie, that a man wants a real woman. Not a plastic one."

Bingo. Column tidbit. I grinned and crossed my arms, waiting for Stacy's response.

"You wouldn't know what it takes to get a man if it bit you in your wrinkled bottom."

"I'll have you know," Betty Larson spoke up. "That Dottie is the most sought after woman at the retirement home. Why, she won last year's beauty contest. You should know, since you interviewed her."

"And I'll win this year's, too." Dottie glared.

"If you're still alive," Mom piped in.

"Don't start that again!" Dottie whirled on her like a duck on a June bug.

"What's this?" Stacy clicked her pen. "Who's dying?"

"Nobody. Certainly not me." Dottie tossed her spool of thread onto the table. "Most likely it's you, or Frank, putting these fake obits in the paper. Anything to sell a few more copies and keep the paper from going under."

Stacy looked confused. "I have no idea what you're talking about." She glanced at me. "Marsha?"

I shrugged, not wanting to give her anything newsworthy, but the more people who knew about the suspicious deaths, the better. "Seems someone is putting people's names in the obits thirty days before the person actually dies. Dottie's name came up last week."

"Why is this the first time I've heard of this?" Stacy speared each woman with her gaze.

"Maybe you don't read your own paper," Mom said. "Danny, quit eavesdropping at the door. If you want something, come on in."

Red-faced, Danny sidled through the door, empty pitcher in his hand. "Mr. Bohan told me to bring this in before it got broke."

I took it from him, feeling pity for the poor shy young man suddenly thrust into the center of attention by a group of fuming females. "Thank you. Now git, before they turn on you."

He disappeared so fast, I thought maybe Houdini played a magic trick. "Times up, ladies. See you next week."

For the next five minutes, there was a flurry of activity as they cleaned up their work and stashed it on a shelf Mom had provided. Stacy stayed and watched for a few minutes before storming out.

It was quite a productive morning. I had gossip on Stacy's fake chest, on Dottie being the belle of the ball, and also on Dottie believing she'd win the pageant at the retirement home again. Yep, this gossip stuff was easy.

Once the women had gone, Mom wiped down the table. "Well, that was interesting. Next week, you can stay in here and I'll mind the store."

"Not on your life." No way did I want to spend two hours with that bunch. Most of them were okay, but Dottie's sharp tongue more than made up for the others.

"So, do you think the obit thing is a ploy to garner sales?"

"What?" I frowned. "No. Do you? Do you really think someone is posting their names and killing them just for publicity? Or… wait." I stared through the window for a moment. "What if…Frank or Stacy are posting the names, but someone else is taking advantage of it."

"That's a thought." Mom tossed the rag she'd used into a basket. "Possible, I suppose, but how would we find out who?" She thrust a finger in the air. "I know! We'll put my name in."

"Are you nuts?" Seriously, she might need committed to the crazy house. "Do you know how dangerous that would be?"

She lowered her voice. "Not if you stay with me every single minute of the thirtieth day."

"So we could both die? No, thanks." I pulled out a chair and sat. "There has to be another way. Besides, Leroy and Duane would never go for it." What if the end came when Lindsey was with us? I couldn't stand to think that way.

"I'm with your daughter on this one." Leroy barged through the back door. "If you're going to talk crazy, at least close the door and window."

"But, honey.—" Mom batted her eyelashes.

Really? Women still did that?

"Don't honey me, Gertie. I'm putting my foot down." Leroy's face reddened. "I told you I'd let you play around with another mystery, since you don't fit the profile of those poor unfortunate women, but I will not allow you to purposely put yourself in harm's way."

Thank you, Lord, that I didn't have to be the one to stand up to my mother this time. She was definitely a force to be reckoned with when riled.

Mom took a deep breath, opened her mouth, closed it again, then finally spoke. "Well, if we don't figure out something, Dottie won't ever have a chance to win her second pageant."

9

The next morning, I sat in the newspaper office, staring at Stacy, who filed her nails. Where was Frank? I glanced at my watch. Ten minutes late.

"He's always late," Stacy said without looking up. "But don't you dare come in late. That'll be the time he shows on time. The man is a bear when mad."

Considering one of my pet peeves was being even two minutes late, I didn't see any danger of me angering Frank that way. I slid the manila folder with the single sheet of gossip around on the table, and envisioned Stacy's reaction when she read the post. If she read it, of course. Somehow I figured she would think that column beneath her. The folder also contained a wonderfully cute advertisement for the store. Lindsey had outdone herself with a picture of a time-out baby standing in a corner and the words "Don't be sent to time-out. Catch the bargains while you can."

"Sorry I'm late." Frank banged through the door and took a seat at the end of the table. "Stacy, what do you have?"

She slid a file to him. "A short write up on that stupid quilter's group, and one on the football team. I'd like to do another one, featuring the coach, after their first game tonight." She shot a simpering smile at me.

The first game was tonight? How could I have forgotten? I never missed any of the home games, especially since Duane and I got together.

"Marsha?" Frank narrowed his eyes. "You must pay attention. We don't want these meetings to go on forever. I have a newspaper to run."

"Sorry." I handed him my file.

He opened it, read, then glanced at Stacy's chest, then at me. I could've sworn I saw the flicker of a smile cross his lips. "Good job. Keep up the good work. See y'all next week." He grabbed the two files and left, all in less than five minutes.

"Then why do we have to mark two hours on our calendar?" I asked.

Stacy shrugged. "Sometimes he's an hour late. Sometimes, he doesn't like what we've written and waits while we fix it. Who knows? We're talking about Frank. Count your blessings it was quick." With those words, she left me alone in the conference room.

I wasn't due at the shop for almost two hours. What in the world would I do with that time? I had no suspects to interrogate and very little clues. Maybe I could badger Bruce into letting something slip.

Grabbing my purse, I headed out of the newspaper office and next door to the police department. In a town the size of River Valley, businesses tended to congregate, thus giving business to each other. In this instance, having the paper next to the police probably made gathering news easier.

The station receptionist lifted her head from her desk, frowned, then waved me through. Oh, how Bruce must love that folks did that for me. That's what happens when people like you. Of course, the receptionist knew from experience I wouldn't leave her alone until she waved me back.

"Good morning, Bruce." His door was open, so I sailed in and planted myself in the chair in front of his desk.

"What do you want?" He crossed his arms and leaned back.

"Is that any way to greet an old friend?" I set my purse on the ground at my feet, catching sight of my very well-worn flip-flops. Maybe I should've taken the extra time I had to go shopping.

"I'm a busy man, Marsha." He fiddled with a stack of papers on his desk.

"Did Duane talk to you about the obituaries?" Might as well get right to the point before he threw me out.

"Are you still on that kick? It's pure coincidence, and nothing more. I have burglaries and vandalism to worry about. I can't go charging around on speculation. And I don't appreciate you sending your bulldog to do your dirty work."

Duane was a bulldog? I sure loved that man. He'd made a promise to me then left an impression. "Well, if Dottie turns up dead, then you'll be sorry, won't you, Officer Fife." I grabbed my purse and lunged to my feet. "Sometimes, you need to listen to the wisdom of other people."

"When I see a wise person, I will."

Ugh. I slammed his door shut behind me. With over an hour before I had to report to work, I decided to visit a little boutique down the street, with the hopes of finding a few things to liven up my wardrobe. Wouldn't Duane be pleased to see me dress as a woman instead of a teenage boy? Yet, the darling man loved me anyway.

A chime sang out as I opened the boutique door. Immediately a myriad of colors and textures assaulted my senses, sending me into overload. A girl with dyed black hair, a piercing in her eyebrow, and another in her lip, kind of smiled, if you can call a grimace a smile, and welcomed me. "Welcome to Heaven's Fashion. I'm Amber. May I help you?"

Somewhat at ease because Heaven was in the store name, I smiled back. "I'm lost. I'd like to dress my age, yet attractive." How could a Goth princess possibly help me?

"Our women's department is over here. We have several sundresses you may like, along with walking shorts, capris, and some blouses on our clearance rack. Warmer clothing is over here." Amber led the way to the back of the store.

These clothes were more to my taste. I riffled through them, almost excited to be shopping, and thankful I'd chosen to go alone. My mother would have me dressing like her. Elastic waistband pants, flowing skirts, and gauzy blouses. "I've never heard of this boutique," I said. "I've only seen the sign in the window. Maybe y'all should put an advertisement in the paper."

She shrugged. "My mom might be interested. She isn't here now."

"Here's my card." I pulled the craft store's business card from the bib of my overalls. "Have your mother call me if she's interested."

"Would you like to try something on?" Her phone rang out a heavy metal tune. "Just a sec." She answered it. "Hey, Danny. I can't talk right now. Got a customer. Call me later."

I hung several outfits over my arm. "I'd like to try these on. Was that Danny Vera?"

"Yes, why?"

"He's helping my stepfather build a room onto our store. A real quiet boy, isn't he?" I stepped back while she unlocked one of the fitting rooms.

"Until you get to know him. But I like my men quiet and broody. Makes them mysterious." She pushed the door open. "Let me know if I can help you with something else."

I wanted to ask Amber more questions about the young man I'd almost run over, but if I'd thought Danny sullen, she took first place. Instead, I marveled at how much better I looked out of my overalls. Why hadn't I noticed how much weight I'd lost? Probably because the overalls were shapeless, and I'd been so busy, I had little time to head to my main source of stress relief. My M&Ms.

Thirty minutes later, and several hundred dollars poorer, I left the store with the beginnings of a new wardrobe. I couldn't wait for Duane to see me in one of the dresses.

I went to work and stashed my bags under the counter, trying to ignore the sound of hammering. Would Leroy and Danny ever finish?

"What's all that?" Mom carried in two glasses of tea.

"I went shopping."

"What are you shipping?" She handed me a glass.

"What?" I guzzled the sweet tea like a woman dying of thirst. I never realized how parched you get when shopping.

"What?"

I stared at her like she'd gone mad, which at moments, wasn't such a long stretch. "Clothes! I went shopping for new clothes."

She remained impassive for a minute, then pulled a wad of cotton out of her ears. "That hammering is going to drive me nuts. You went shopping? Thank the good Lord!" She pulled out one of my new dresses. "This is lovely. So glad you finally took my advice."

"Danny's girlfriend works there. Strange girl, but nice." I tied my apron around my waist and glanced around the store to see what crafts needed to be made. Still crowded. Moving to the order book, I flipped to the first page. Somebody wants a leprechaun? How was I supposed to make that? I pointed at the order. "Did you take this?"

"Who else would take it?"

"Any ideas?" Mom might own the store, but most of the crafts were a result of my two hands.

"A time-out doll that looks like a leprechaun. Sew a green outfit, go to the party store for a hat, and glue on some orange hair and beard. There, you have it."

Sure, easy for her to say. I searched our book of patterns for a toddler boy's short suit. St. Patrick's day wasn't for almost a year. Why would these folks want one now? Sometimes, I thought Mom had a personal agenda: to kill me. Good thing I had a couple of time-out babies in the closet from a canceled order. All I'd have to do would be to change the clothes.

"Those people are having some kind of Irish party. You know me, I don't ask a lot of questions." Mom looked out the backdoor. "Who's that woman?"

And some people suffered from delusions. I joined her. "That's Darla from the newspaper." What was she doing here? I opened the door and stepped outside. "Darla? Is something wrong with my column?"

"No. I'm here to check on my son. You slave drivers have him working all day."

"Danny's your son?"

"Didn't I just say that?" She stomped over to where he sat on a folding stool, nursing a glass of tea. That boy could keep Lipton in business all by himself.

"Don't embarrass me, Mom." Danny stood. "I told you I get off at five, same as any other worker. Same as you."

"But you're only twenty-four. That's too young for such long hours." She patted his cheek. "You should be out having fun. And not with that girl you're seeing. Someone…else."

Interesting. Momma didn't seem to like Amber. Once you got past the piercings and dark clothes, she didn't seem too bad. Besides, if I'd learned anything from being a mother, it was that the child would gravitate to the very thing I wanted her away from.

"Leave it be!" Danny threw the red plastic cup that had once held his drink. It landed at his mother's feet, splashing the buff-colored pumps she wore. "Don't you tell me to do enough things?"

"Nothing that doesn't need doing, Danny." Darla straightened her shoulders and marched away, leaving the rest of us silent, and with our mouths hanging open.

"Go on, boy." Leroy wiped his hands on a rag that looked as if it had been run over by a truck. "Your mama needs you. This room will be here tomorrow. Now that the boards are all cut, we can set up the walls in the morning."

Thank goodness. If the weather held, they should be finished in a week. Hopefully by the next quilting get-together. Too many more days of hammering, and I might just nail my head to the floor.

Danny followed his mother, and Mom and I went inside. "Seems kind of early for her to pick him up, doesn't it?" Especially considering it was only a little past one.

"He's twenty-four, for crying out loud. Not a child. You had a baby by his age." Mom grabbed the broom and started sweeping. "Women who coddle their offspring make me furious."

"It's really none of our business." I searched the shelves for a bolt of emerald green fabric. Nada. "Do you have any green fabric at your house? I really don't want to go to the store."

"I might." She leaned on the broom handle, crushing the bristles. "I told Leroy that come this summer, we could buy an RV. You sure you're okay with that? If you'd set a wedding date, then I'd have a better idea of when we could actually leave."

"What difference does that make?"

"Because, once you're Duane's problem, I don't need to follow you around on your crime-solving adventures."

10

First game of the season. I sat on the bleachers, prepared for the weather in long pants, a blanket folded under me to cushion the hard metal seat, a serving of nachos beside me, and a cold diet soda in my hand. It might still be a bit warm during the day, but the nights had a tendency to cool off. Maybe I should focus on shopping for some stylish jeans and long-sleeved tees.

Duane turned and scanned the bleachers. Finding me, he waved. I gave him a thumbs-up, trying to ignore Stacy, who grinned beside him like some deranged cheerleader. There to take notes on the game, I was sure, once she got finished ogling my man.

So be it. Duane either loved me or he didn't, and I was pretty sure he did. Mom was right. Life was too short to be spent on jealousy when there was no reason.

Lindsey strolled by with one of her friends. They stopped along the fence. Most likely to stare at River Valley's quarterback, Bobby. Lindsey wouldn't tell me why they broke up, and I didn't ask. She'd tell me in due time.

Danny and Amber shuffled by, the bored look on their faces exactly like so many of their generation. Young people seemed to think it was a cool look. That young man acted like a teenager and looked like a teenager. Finding out he was twenty-four came as a shock. But, if the one time I saw him and Darla together was any indication, the woman refused to loosen the apron strings.

The ball was airborne: River Valley Copperheads received and made their first down. I picked up my nachos, desperately trying to enjoy the taste, knowing they'd land right on my hips. A girl had to break her diet once in a while, and football season was as good an excuse as anything.

Interception! The Copperheads were going to have to get it together if they wanted to win. I leaped to my feet, yelling, sending my dinner sliding between the bleacher seats to the dirt below. Now, I'd have to climb under there to pick up my garbage. I pouted and plopped back to a sitting position, trying to locate the spilled nachos through the space between the boards.

"The game is on the field," Mom said as she and Leroy took their seats next to me. "We're late." She smiled and gave Leroy a glance I'd rather not interpret.

"It's still the first quarter. We gave the ball away."

"We'll get it back." Leroy situated himself on his bleacher chair and set a small cooler at his feet.

"How'd you get that in here?" The watchdogs at the gate prohibited anyone bringing in their own food and drinks.

"I have connections." He winked.

"I lost my supper. Do you have anything in there to spare?" I kept my gaze locked on the blue and white cooler.

"Your mom has hot dogs in her purse."

Mom pulled out a foil wrapped dog from the quilted bag slung over her shoulder. "I figured you'd be hungry. You always are."

"You know me so well." I unwrapped the dog and took a bite of spicy mustard and relish. Just the way I liked my hot dogs.

"You dropping your nachos was God's way of telling you not to eat garbage." Mom handed Leroy his own wrapped meal.

Somehow, I doubted God would go to such extremes, but Mom was right. I needed to eat healthier, and chips drowned in canned cheese sauce didn't qualify. But they sure were good.

By the end of the first quarter, the Copperheads were up by one touchdown, and my stomach hurt from two hot dogs and a bag of chips. When would I learn to pace myself?

Bobby leaned across the fence and talked to Lindsey until Duane called him away. Lindsey turned toward the bleachers, a wide smile on her face. Hmmm. I decided to head under the bleachers to collect my napkin and nacho box before asking my daughter why the grin.

After collecting the trash from Mom and Leroy, I headed down the bleachers and to the nearest trash can. Under the bleachers, I scanned the area for a stick or rock big enough to scrape up my mess. No way was I touching the nachos with my bare hands. Not after they'd been lying in the dirt for thirty minutes.

"I told her I didn't want to, but she won't leave me alone."

I froze, trying to discern where the voice came from. It was a young man, of that I was certain.

A girl answered. "You need to stand up for yourself. I don't know what it is that has you so bothered, but no one should be able to dictate your actions. Not at your age, at least."

A sense of de ja vu came over me. During the last mystery I'd been involved in, I'd found myself under the bleachers eavesdropping. Maybe the police should take up this line of investigating.

"Hey, Mrs. Steele. What are you doing?"

I sighed and closed my eyes, recognizing the voice of the mascot, Timmy Weldon. Why wasn't he on the field? Now, I'd learn nothing more tonight. "Hi, Timmy." The voices had stopped. I scooped up the nachos the best I could and climbed through the poles holding up the bleachers. "Good game, isn't it?"

"Yeah, but I had to take a break. This costume is hot." He wobbled his head, making the fangs on the snake head dip closer to my face. I knew his voice, but the mask effectively hid his identity. "Are you under here spying on the kids making out?"

"What? No." Kids were making out? Where?

"There's always several, Mrs. Steele. You should keep your eyes open." Timmy gave a wave of one scaly paw, despite snakes not having hands, and left.

I glanced around the surrounding area, trying to determine whose conversation I had been listening to. Timmy was right. There were at least four different couples in lip-locks. Not wanting to know any more, I headed back to Mom and Leroy. Wait a minute! That was Lindsey.

"What in the world are you doing?"

Lindsey jumped back from the boy she was kissing as if stung. "Mom?"

I crossed my arms and narrowed my eyes. "Explain, and you…" I pointed at the boy I didn't know. "Can leave."

"You're embarrassing me," Lindsey hissed. "It doesn't mean anything. I'm trying to make Bobby jealous."

"By kissing under the bleachers like common trash?" Lord, save me from teenagers. "I thought you were a good girl." Had I jinxed her by telling everyone my daughter was good?

"I am a good girl. We were only kissing! What are you doing under here?"

"Picking up garbage."

She shook her head. "I have the weirdest mother in the world. Why can't you be normal? You were under here snooping."

That set me back. What was normal, anyway? "Not on purpose. Who all was under here, anyway? I heard something."

She groaned. "I am not going to snitch." With a toss of her hair, she stomped to the edge of the stairs.

With her flouncing off, I'd lost any chance of knowing whose conversation I'd overheard. I shrugged. Most likely some kid who didn't want to do what his parents said, and an evil girl out to mislead him. Spirits low, I sank down next to Mom. My daughter had shattered all my illusions about her. What kind of girl made out under the bleachers during a crowded football game? Just to make another boy jealous!

I watched the second quarter under a depressed fog. Even my wave to Duane, when he turned, was half-hearted. No doubt he'd ask me about it later. I watched as Timmy hopped along the sidelines, tripping over invisible obstacles, and harassing the cheerleaders. At least someone was having fun.

"What's got your knickers in a twist?" Mom handed me a bottle of water.

"I caught Lindsey kissing a boy under the bleachers. I'm devastated. It feels like someone ripped my heart out and filled my stomach with cement."

"Don't be so dramatic. Everyone makes out under the bleachers at some time during high school."

"I never did." Really? Everyone?

Mom patted my knee. "Sorry, sweetie, but you weren't real popular in school. You've always been a bit...weird. I was always surprised that Duane dated you. Now, I bet he spent some time under the bleachers before dating you."

And I intended to ask him first thing why he never took me! I bolted to my feet and stomped down the stairs, eliciting some frustrated glances from the other spectators. Making my way to the fence, I waited until half-time, then waved Duane over. "Why haven't you ever taken me to make out under the bleachers?"

"Excuse me?" His brow wrinkled, and he glanced over his shoulder to the ball team. "Do I have to answer that now? I need to talk to the team."

"No, but I expect an answer after the game."

"Wait there." He sprinted to the team, said a few words, then dashed back to me. He leaped the fence and grabbed my hand. "I've been wanting to do this for years."

I yelped as he dragged me along behind him. "I didn't intend for us to do this now. I only wanted to know why we never did."

He pulled me to a secluded spot and into his arms. "Because I thought you'd slap my face." He wrapped his hands in my hair and planted a heavy kiss on my lips. He kept it up until my breath came in gasps and my legs swooned. If this was what making out under the bleachers was like, I was going to kill Lindsey.

"Way to go, Coach!" A young man strolled by, his arm around a girl's shoulders.

My face heated as hot as my blood, and I pulled away.

Duane gave me a crooked grin. "Was it everything you thought it would be?"

Heaven. I struggled to breathe, and nodded.

After another kiss, Duane pulled me back to the fence. "Woman, you are a distraction." He grinned and jumped back to his team, who all gave him high-fives.

If I weren't the one writing the paper's gossip column, I'd bet there'd be a blurb in next week's paper about us. Thankfully, no one, other than the kids, seemed to know what we'd been up to.

Despite the race of my pulse, I sat with a grin on my face for the rest of the game. Whenever Mom asked what was wrong, I'd giggle and say nothing. Not that she believed me, but the interaction with Duane was our little secret. Our steamy little secret.

"Dottie seems to be testing the waters," Mom said. "She told me today that she plans on staying home alone on the thirtieth day. Said if somebody wanted her dead, they could fight her over it, because she didn't plan to just roll over and let them take her out."

"That's a crazy bunch of women you hang out with." Leroy uncapped another bottle of water. "Here, Marsha, you look a little flushed."

I accepted the water with a thank you. When he kept watching me, I guzzled about half the bottle and prayed I wouldn't drown. Was this the subterfuge most teenagers went through? The normal ones, at least?

"I don't hang out with Dottie." Mom glowered at him. "We can't stand each other. Can barely tolerate being in the same room together for longer than a minute."

The Copperheads scored another touchdown, bringing them up by six points and the spectators to their feet. My water bottle rolled down the bleachers, splashing the feet of everyone in its path.

"You are a walking disaster." Mom scuttled after it, retrieved the now empty bottle, and handed it back to me.

I shrugged. "At least I'm not going to be the prime suspect when Dottie winds up dead."

11

Mom didn't talk to me for the rest of the night, despite my apology to her and to God for my petty remark. But, she'd kept her lips clamped as tight as a kid given medicine. I took a sip of sweet tea and popped up the foot rest on my lawn chair. It was after ten p.m., but I couldn't go to bed until Lindsey got home, so I decided to enjoy a calm autumn evening in the Ozark foothills.

Considering my senses still tingled from Duane's kiss under the bleachers, I refused to let anything mar the evening. Especially since after the game, he invited me to join him in the same spot at half time in two weeks. I sure had missed out on a lot by being shy in high school. Even with my then boyfriend, Duane. He'd respected my wishes and let me keep him at arm's length.

Maybe that was why he left so soon after graduation. I took another sip of tea. Dwelling on the past never accomplished anything, though. Duane and I were engaged. All I needed was a wedding date. Maybe in the spring. May would be a beautiful month for a wedding. An outdoor wedding.

The ringing of my cell phone interrupted one of the few times I actually spent on wedding planning. I set my glass on a nearby café table and fished the phone out of my pocket.

"Hello?"

"You think you're so slick, eavesdropping under the bleachers," the electronically modified voice said. "Stop putting your nose where it doesn't belong." Click.

Well, drat. Here we went again with the threats.

Six months ago, I'd almost single-handedly been responsible for the arrest of the women's ministry leader. Sure, she hadn't actually meant to kill anyone, but poisoning them so they would forget certain details was just as bad. And one of those episodes had resulted in a death. It was time to dig out my twenty-two pistol and Tazer. Duane would not be pleased.

Maybe I could add to the gossip column that I'd received a threat? By doing so, I could possibly drag the murderer out of hiding, instead of dragging the investigation on for the rest of Dottie's thirty days. Of course, by doing so, I'd be increasing the risk to myself.

Me or Dottie? That was a tough one.

I picked up my glass of tea and watched as Mom's bedroom light flickered off. I'd miss her and Leroy when they left to travel America. One more reason to set a date before they left. Then, I'd have

Duane and Lindsey to keep me company, not to mention full control of the store.

Thwack. The glass in my hand exploded.

I knew that sound and dove to the ground, taking what cover I could under my chair. Slivers of glass pierced my hand. Blood glued leaves and dry grass to my sliced palm.

Either someone was a very good shot, or a very poor one. I trembled, realizing how close I'd come to dying. I leaned more toward a very good shot. Otherwise, why bother with the phone call? They could have just put a bullet through my head, and I would have been none the wiser.

For several minutes, I sat and shook like an old Chihuahua before figuring the shooter had left. I dialed Bruce's personal number.

"What?" From the tone of his voice, I gathered I'd woken him.

"Someone just took a shot at me." My throat clogged with tears as the adrenaline started to wear off. "I'm bleeding."

"Where are you?"

"In front of my cottage hiding behind a lawn chair."

Silence. "Uh, that isn't much protection. Get in the house." Click.

I crawled through my front door and closed it, then dialed Duane's number. By this time, I sobbed so hard my words were unintelligible.

"I'm on my way." My hero.

I still sat on the floor blubbering when Bruce and Duane arrived, both bursting into the cottage at the same time. Duane immediately went to his knees and took my bleeding hand in his. "What happened?"

I shook my head and lunged into his arms.

"She said she was shot at." Bruce stood in the doorway. "I'll look around out here while you take care of that hand. If it's a bullet wound, she'll need to go to the hospital. We have to record things like that."

"Shot at?" Duane pulled me to my feet and over to the sink. "Talk to me."

I sniffed and wiped my face on my sleeve. "First, I got a phone call telling me not to eavesdrop, then someone shot my glass out of my hand."

"Who called?" Bruce whipped out his ever present pad of paper and a pencil.

"The voice was disguised." I hissed through clenched teeth as Duane thrust my hand under the faucet. "I was sitting there planning our wedding."

"You were?" A grin spread across Duane's face.

"I'm thinking May."

"Sounds perfect." Once the blood and dirt was washed away, Duane dabbed my hand with a paper towel and started picking out bits of glass. "Of course, tomorrow would work for me, too."

"Don't be silly. Mom would kill us."

"Maybe if she knew what was going on." Mom pushed past Bruce, tightening her terry robe over a long flannel nightgown. Lucky Leroy.

"There's been a shooting, Mrs. Bohan. Please step aside and let me do my job." Bruce bristled with importance.

"Marsha!" She shoved past him, causing him to drop his pad, then continued to my side where she yanked my hand out of Duane's. "Who shot you? Are you okay? Why isn't an ambulance here?" She glared.

Obviously, she was no longer angry with me. "We don't know yet, yes, and we didn't call one. Someone shot the glass I was holding, and I got cut." My knees wobbled. "There's no need for an ambulance."

If not for Duane's quick response to scooping me in his arms, I would have fallen. Seconds later, he'd laid me on the sofa, pillow under my head, and placed a colorful afghan across me. Then, he resumed work on my hand.

I met Mom's hurt gaze over his head. Her eyes shimmered with unshed tears. For so many years, she'd taken care of me. Then, I married Robert, he died, and Mom had me back. Now, she stood aside while Duane took over. How would I feel when that happened with Lindsey? "Mom, I'd love a glass of tea. Almost getting shot has made me thirsty. Do you mind?"

"I'll make you a fresh pot." She bustled back to the main house.

"That was sweet." Duane lifted my hand to his lips and gently kissed the palm. "She was having a hard time not bandaging this hand. I could have let her, but, I needed to do this, too."

"Mom?" Lindsey entered the room, eyes wide, and furtive glances at Bruce. "What did you do?"

Why did she always assume that whatever happened to me was my fault? This definitely wasn't. Well, maybe it was, considering I spent time contemplating a murder and warning another potential victim. But, I would stick with my story. "Nothing. I was waiting for you."

"It's not my curfew for another twenty minutes."

"I was only enjoying the nice night."

"Stop badgering your mother." Duane gently sat my freshly wrapped hand on my stomach and stood to face Lindsey. "Most of the time, I butt out of things between the two of you, but your mother was shot at and injured, and all you're worried about is her keeping tabs on you. I may only be your uncle, soon to be your stepfather, but I will not allow you to speak to your mother that way."

Lindsey stared at him for a moment, eyes flashing, then flounced down the hall to her room. Since she'd been so young when her father died, she'd never had a man correct her behavior before. Thankfully, I rarely had to discipline her. But lately, I hardly recognized the teenage girl down the hall.

"Thank you." I motioned for Duane to bend down. After kissing him, I smiled. "I'm exhausted. Do you mind?"

He smoothed the hair away from my face. "Not at all. Are you staying on the sofa or do you want me to help you to bed?"

"Mom would be scandalized by you taking me there, but the bed sounds lovely." I sat up, and although I was now perfectly capable of making it to my room on my own, I relished the gallant gesture from my knight. Assuring him I'd be fine, though, I stayed on the sofa. Minutes later, I kissed him again, promised to call him when I woke in the morning, and waved him away.

Mom had never returned with my tea. I suspected Leroy waylaid her and told her the truth about my wanting a glass. With my good hand, I pulled the afghan up under my chin and closed my eyes. Cleopatra, my German Shepard, laid her head on my hip. "Where were you, girl? You could've warned me that a madman lurked in the bushes." I scratched behind her ears. A not-so-small measure of guilt over how little time I'd spent with her assailed me. Yet, she loved me with every wag of her tail.

Wait. Cleo had been nowhere in sight while I enjoyed my tea and explored what little I knew of the mystery. I rolled back over. Twigs and dirt covered her coat. "Had someone tied you up? Is that why you weren't around?" I'd thought she was off, nose to the ground, to scare up a squirrel. I'd been so preoccupied with my thoughts I hadn't noticed my companion wasn't lying at my feet.

What if she'd never come back home? What if the shooter and done away with her?

I fell to my knees, wrapped my arms around her neck, and buried my face. "Girl, I thought you were a tough watchdog. You need to stick around."

Lindsey strolled back through, two oatmeal cookies and a glass of milk in her hand. "So, what did you do to your hand?"

"Cut in on a glass." Was there any way to keep Lindsey from finding out the whole truth?

"Can't find anything." Bruce held up a bullet casing. "Sniper rifle. You were lucky." He slipped it into his pocket. "Come down to the station tomorrow to fill out the report, okay? I'm going back to bed."

Lindsey watched him go as she took a bite of her cookie. Then, she turned her narrow gaze to me. "I don't want to know." She whirled and marched out of sight.

Suit herself. Since I was awake and no longer felt as if the ground heaved under my feet, I tucked my throbbing hand close to my stomach and moved to the bedroom. Cleo's nails tapped on the wood floor behind me. There'd be no more forest wandering for her. Not for a while. For both of our safety, I needed her close.

Through my bedroom window, I could see Mom's kitchen light still on. What if I went over there to pass some time? Was she still angry about my comment at the game, or Duane's sending her away? I decided to chance it. There were moments in every woman's life when she needed her mother. This was one of mine.

"Going to Mom's!" Opening the front door, I peered both ways into the night, then scuttled to the main house as fast as I could. Cleo kept so close to my legs, she threatened to trip me several times.

The screen door squeaked as I opened it. Mom glanced up from the table, jumped to her feet, and came running. She wrapped me so tight in her arms, I thought she'd smother me. "I'm so sorry, Marsha. I have a sharp tongue. I should cut it off and feed it to the cat."

"No." I shook my head. "I'm the one saying mean things. I'm so sorry."

Mom led me to the table. "Do you want some coffee? Tea?"

"Just water, thanks." I rested my hand on the table, wishing for something strong to kill the pain, but knowing how dopey I got while on pain meds.

"Do you really think I'll be the main suspect if Dottie dies?" Mom filled a glass with ice cubes and water from the refrigerator. "Because, that would make it seem as if I'd killed the other two women. I might have a sharp tongue, but I'm no killer."

12

I stared across the desk at Bruce and cradled my bandaged hand in my lap. "Are you willing to accept the fact that Dottie Baker is in danger?"

"I'm willing to accept the fact you're on to something, yes."

"Come on, Bruce. Dottie needs police protection."

He reached for a stained coffee mug and eyed me over the rim. "She hasn't been shot at and threatened. You have." He took a sip and set the cup down. "We have the bare minimum of police here, Marsha. Me, and a recently hired part-timer. Are you willing to give up your protection for Dottie's?"

That was a tough question. It shouldn't have been. I should have leaped to my feet, fist in the air, and shouted, "Yes, give Dottie the protection." Instead, I remained quiet. Dottie had a few more weeks before her deadline. My danger was immediate. "Can't you temporarily have some officers come down from Little Rock?"

"Everyone has cut back on personnel." Bruce leaned back in his chair. "We may have had our differences in the past, and you may make me want to shoot myself on occasion, but I'll do my best to keep you walking this earth."

His words warmed my heart. He did care. I blinked back tears. "Thank you."

"Don't start blubbering." He rolled back in his chair and crashed into the wall behind him. "I can't stand crying women."

"I'm leaving." Sewing and crafts might be difficult to manage, but I could at least work the register at the store. I'd also decided to add last night's happenings to my gossip post. Nothing better to divert attention from me as the writer, than by putting in something about myself.

I headed down the street toward the coffee shop. A late night warranted a big Venti-sized coffee. My hand had throbbed into the wee hours of the morning and kept me from a deep sleep. I used my hip to push open the door, then stepped inside, relieved to see Duane wasn't interviewing with Stacy.

Instead of heading straight to Country Gifts from Heaven, I sat at a small table outside the coffee shop and watched the cars drive past. I'd promised Duane last night I wouldn't go anywhere alone. Sitting in plain sight of River Valley's residents definitely wouldn't count as alone. Probably everyone who drove past could tell you what time they'd seen me and what I was wearing.

I ran my good hand down the dark jeans I wore. Definitely better than my overalls. Paired with the cranberry sweater set, I looked better than I had in a long time, and of course, Duane was nowhere around. Being a Saturday, I'd hoped to run into him at the coffee shop. I glanced at my watch. Nine o'clock. Most likely he'd be in soon. My man was as regular as clock work, and if we hadn't made a date for Saturday morning coffee at my place, it was always at the coffee shop.

A Ford 150 truck cruised into a space in front of me. Duane climbed out, giving me a glimpse of scuffed cowboy boots, then long denim clad legs, before the ripple of muscles through a black tee, as he closed the truck door. He sauntered over to me and kissed my cheek. "Why are you sitting out here in view of everybody?"

"You told me not to be alone. This is as public as I could get."

"I'll get our drinks and be right back. You look great." After glancing up and down the street, he shoved through the shop doors.

His worry made me nervous, but I could be shot inside as well as outside. At least out here, there was less tendency for an innocent bystander to get in the way. My skin crawled with invisible bugs as I tensed and waited for something, anything, out of the ordinary.

Duane returned with our coffees and sat next to me. "Your mom is watching out the window."

"I know." I waved and watched her pull back behind the display of quilts. "She's worried about it."

"We all are." He took my hand in his. "After the last time… well, I'd rather not think about that."

"Other than Nina coming to ask for my help, I didn't go looking for this. But then, seeing Dottie's name…well," I sucked on my straw. I really had no idea what to say. This case came to me. None of my family members were being fingered for a crime they didn't commit. I had absolutely no reason to be involved, other than a woman's cry for help. A woman I'd failed to keep safe.

"I understand, and I know why you feel you need to solve this."

Did he? Because I certainly didn't. I'd done very little sleuthing, come to think of it, yet someone still tried to kill me.

"Did you fill out the report at the police department?" Duane pulled his gaze from the road and fixed it on my face.

"Yes, right before coming here. Bruce is actually starting to believe something fishy is going on."

"Good. Before you head to work, I want you to have your hand checked out." Duane stood and pulled me to my feet. "I cleaned it as well as I could, but not as well as a doctor."

"Fine, but just take me to the Little Clinic in the drug store. There's no point in sitting for hours at the doctor's office or urgent care." Usually I balked at anything to do with seeing a doctor, but considering how much my hand throbbed, I was actually hoping for some pain meds.

Duane escorted me down the block to the drug store. I'd never visited the clinic inside, but townspeople have raved at the convenience. Ten minutes later, I sat in a small back room with a smiling woman wearing a white lab coat.

"Mrs. Steele, what have you managed to do to yourself?" She carefully unwrapped my hand and tsk-tsked. After flushing the cuts with some type of solution, she put on a pair of magnifying glasses and picked up some tweezers. "Whoever cleaned this did a good job, but missed a few little strays. Once I get these picked out, I'll give you a shot of antibiotics, a prescription for pain meds, and send you on your way. Butterfly Band-Aids should be enough. I don't think you need stitches."

Wonderful. People were right. How nice not to sit for hours in an emergency room or urgent care for something minor.

"There." She rewrapped my hand. "Try to take it easy for a couple of days. Don't use your hand, and you should heal up just fine."

"Thank you." I took the prescription and headed back to the waiting area where Duane waited. "Looks like I've got a couple of days to sit around on pain meds and rest."

"Good. You could use it."

"Mom won't be happy. This will leave her short-handed." At least I'd be back to work by next Thursday, when the quilting group met again. "And being stuck at home will put a damper on collecting gossip."

"Let's catch some lunch while your prescription is filled." Duane escorted me down the road to Wanda's diner. Normally, all the walking along Main Street had no effect on me, but that day, my body dragged. Exhaustion covered me like a humid blanket. Sitting down sounded like heaven.

Once inside, I slid with a sigh into a booth and laid my head back. "Order me a BLT on wheat with avocado, french fries on the side, and a diet soda. I'm beat."

"Maybe I should take you home and bring your prescription to you." Duane's eyes focused with concern on mine.

"No, I still need to eat before taking a pill. Otherwise, my stomach—"

"How dare you!" Stacy marched to our table and planted her palms flat with a slap onto the Formica top.

I pushed back against the red vinyl seatback. "What?"

"Your column and my chest. How dare you post something so outrageous?" Her face turned so scarlet, I feared for her blood pressure.

"Need I remind you that it's a gossip column?" Wanda, owner of the diner, set our drinks in front of us and took a few steps back, clearly more interested in Stacy's tirade than in retrieving our lunch. "People don't take it serious. They only read it for fun."

"You had implants?" Wanda asked. "Can't hardly tell." She stabbed a finger at Stacy's chest. "Are they real?"

Stacy's mouth opened and closed like a fish, before her steely gaze swung back to me. "Don't touch me. Watch it, Marsha. You're treading on thin ice." She tried to stomp away on her four inch heels, but only succeeded in wobbling a bit on her way to the door.

"This is why you can't be left alone for even five minutes," Duane pointed out. "Stacy is not someone you want to make your enemy."

I shrugged. "We were never friends to begin with."

"Uh-oh. That's my cue." Wanda motioned her head toward the door where Dottie barged inside. "She looks madder than a hatter, and I'm not in the mood."

Dottie made a beeline for our table and scooted in beside Duane. She took a deep breath and expelled through her nose, before folding her hands on the tabletop, staring with wide eyes at me. "Marsha, Marsha, Marsha. Is your mother the new gossip columnist?"

Not exactly the question I'd expected. "No, ma'am, I'm pretty sure she isn't. Why?"

"Someone posted about me being on a dead line, no pun intended, and how I believed I'd win the retirement pageant again this year. Who else but your mother would post that?" Her penciled eyebrows moved to peaks.

"Well…" I took a sip of my soda, enjoying the cool carbonation before answering. "The quilting group were all present when you were talking about the pageant." They were there, weren't they? I couldn't remember for sure. I looked to Duane for help, but he suddenly became interested in the burger Wanda sat in front of him.

"Hmmm." She tapped a fingernail the color of poppies against her dentist-whitened teeth. "I didn't think any of them knew about the obituary, but anything's possible. Especially with the fuss your mother was making."

"Dottie, I think you may want to talk to Bruce." Duane came out of his burger stupor and laid a hand over her wrinkled one.

Her face flushed like a young girl's. I grinned. My man had that effect on women. "I don't care to speak to that man."

"But, darling, he's beginning to feel concerned about your safety as well as the rest of us." Duane gave her a tender smile. "For me. Talk to him."

"You, sir, are a good-looking rascal with a silk tongue. Flattery drips from your lips." Dottie slid her hand free. "But you know as well as I do that our esteemed Officer Barnett is not capable of keeping a kitten safe, much less a feisty old lady. He even locked Nina in jail, little good it did, though." She shook her head, then stood. "No, I'll take my chances. Since Gertie and Marsha have warned me, I'll keep my eyes peeled."

"You mean...you believe us?" I couldn't believe the masquerade she'd put on.

"I'd be silly not to. No, Gertie and I love to spar with each other. We've been doing it for years." She tossed a twenty-dollar bill on the table. "Lunch is on me. You two young people are good for an old woman's soul."

I slid from the booth and motioned for Duane to stay before I followed Dottie outside. "Someone shot at me last night." I held up my bandaged hand. "Luckily, they only got the glass. Please, be careful. And when that day number thirty comes, I'll spend it with you at the mall. We'll stay in a public place. You're right. The River Valley police can't keep us safe."

Dottie patted my cheek. "You're a doll, and I'd love a day at the mall with you. But sweetie, when it's my time, it's my time. I'm an old woman. When God calls me home, I'll go."

13

I understand her words, but realized that as much as I loved my heavenly Father, I wasn't ready to go to that mansion in the sky just yet. I waved as she climbed into a cotton-candy pink Cadillac and backed out of the parking spot without looking.

A man I didn't recognize, laid on his horn while flipping Dottie a gesture no gentleman would use toward a lady. He stuck his head out of the window. "Stupid old drivers! Ought to all be euthanized." He roared into the spot she'd vacated, then got out of his truck.

I stepped aside as the barrel-chested man barged into the diner. Duane came out a few seconds later, a paper bag in his hands. "You didn't eat, so I had Wanda bag it for you. I want you to sit in my truck while I pick up your prescription."

"Do you mind dropping me off at the store, then picking me back up? I need to let Mom know I won't be working today." Thankfully, tomorrow was Sunday and the store would be closed.

Duane dropped me off at Country Gifts, then left. I knew he'd be back within fifteen minutes, so I pushed through the door and struggled not to look as tired as I felt. "Mom?"

"Back here."

I headed to the back room.

Mom stood at the window, hands on her hips. "That kid, Danny, works hard, I'll give him that. But sometimes, he just sits and stares at the ground like he doesn't have a lick of sense."

I stepped beside her. Sure enough, Danny sat on a folding stool and stared at the ground between his feet. "Maybe he's resting from all his work."

"Maybe. But something heavy rests on that boy's mind." Mom turned. "How's the hand?"

"Duane took me to the clinic. They cleaned it out, gave me a prescription for pain and antibiotics, and told me to rest for a couple of days. So, he's coming to pick me up, and I'll be at home the rest of the weekend. Can you manage?"

"You bet. Go home and rest. I'll check on you later." Mom gave me a hug and then a gentle nudge toward the door. "Love you, sweetie."

Duane was just pulling up to the curb when I stepped outside. I climbed into the truck cab and closed my eyes. Duane patted my shoulder, then handed me a pill and a sip from his water bottle. "You'll be home and in bed within ten minutes."

It wasn't just my hand hurt that gave me pain and dragged me down, but that someone wanted to kill me. Add in that Dottie's life was also in danger, and I didn't know which way to turn to protect either one of us.

Last time, the murderer had been someone I saw on a regular basis: A member of high-standing in the church. She'd been head of the women's ministry. I ran through my mind everyone I knew that could possibly wire a house to blow up. I didn't know anyone.

Duane pulled the truck to the back of Mom's house, making the distance to the cottage less. He thought of everything. By this time, my legs were starting to feel like rubber because of the pain meds, and I happily leaned on Duane's arm while he half-carried me into the cottage.

"Sofa or bed?" He pushed open the door.

"Sofa, with the remote close by."

"You got it." Duane settled me on the sofa, propped pillows behind my back, then headed to the kitchen. A few minutes later, he returned with a water bottle from the refrigerator. "Where's Lindsey?"

"I have no idea." She'd been sleeping when I'd left the house that morning. "Maybe she's still in bed."

"I'll check." He headed down the hall, returning seconds later. "Nope. I'll text her to come home and take care of you until your mom gets off work. I have some football stuff to do."

"I'm not dying, Duane." Yes, my hand felt like it was killing me, and I loved all the attention he poured on me, but I didn't need a full-time babysitter for a few cuts. "I'm going to sleep, then watch some television. I'll see you later."

He kissed me and left. I rolled over and gave in to the pain meds.

*

Loud voices woke me. Not angry, just voices trying to speak over the sound of a power tool. Tossing aside the afghan I'd covered with, I shuffled to the window and parted the curtains.

"I'll tell you right now, son." Leroy wiped his face with a stained bandanna. "A man has to own up to his mistakes."

"What mistake?" Danny jerked, dropping the hammer. "How did you find out?"

"The fact you nailed those two boards in the wrng place! Are you asleep? I can see your mistake with my own two eyes." Leroy shook his head. "You swore you didn't smoke any of that loco weed, but sometimes I wonder."

Danny visibly relaxed. Yep. Someday, that boy and I were going to have a long chat so I could ferret out his secrets.

I stepped onto my tiny porch, more like a stoop really. "Leroy, what are y'all doing?"

"Sorry, sweetie. Didn't know you were home. I guess we're making quite the racket out here." Leroy clicked off the sander. "Your mother wanted the back porch rails smoothed and repainted. Since the back room is almost finished at the store, and she complained of a headache, I thought I'd use Danny for another hour or two. He doesn't mind the extra money, do you, boy?"

Danny rolled his eyes and shrugged. "My mom is probably pacing the floor right about now. If I'm not home when she gets there, she starts to worry."

"A man your age shouldn't have to worry too much about that. It isn't good to rely on your mother too much at your age." Leroy pointed at a stack of wood beside the back porch. "Check those for warped pieces, then go on home."

Obviously, I wasn't going to get anymore rest. I moved back into the house, grabbed my bag of M&Ms from the cookie jar, and settled in front of the television with a chick flick. I might as well try to enjoy the rest of my day.

Leroy might be noisy, but I felt a whole lot better knowing I wasn't alone. The afternoon passed with the sound of sawing from outside and vows of love from the TV. Occasionally, I'd glance at the clock to check the time, wondering where Lindsey was, but at the almost tender age of sixteen, she flew off the handle when I asked too many questions. She had a dinner curfew and a night time curfew, and woe to the one who checked on her before those times.

The closer she got to becoming an adult, the more of a stranger she became. Was every teenage girl such a nightmare? Last mystery we'd been involved in, Lindsey couldn't wait to help me solve it. Neither could Mom. Maybe that's why I was getting nowhere fast. The three Callahan women weren't together.

I sat up and grabbed my cell phone off the coffee table, then texted Mom and Lindsey for a meeting right after supper. With it being Saturday night, my daughter might balk a bit, but I was hoping she'd be thrilled at helping us brainstorm.

Seconds later, I received a text from my daughter saying, 'If I have to' and one from my mother saying she'd bring cake and coffee. Maybe I should have texted her first, then relayed her message to Lindsey. Cake could sway the toughest opponent.

The hours until the meeting time of seven o'clock dragged, despite Duane bringing pizza and Lindsey actually coming home in time to eat. Since she loved her uncle, conversation wasn't stilted as I've heard it could be with prospective step-parents. But…she did get a glint in her eye when he spoke to her in a gruff voice about her attitude. How would she act if we decided to have another child?

"You're quiet tonight. Is your hand hurting?" Duane bit into a slice of meat lover's pizza.

"No, just thinking." I smiled at Lindsey. "Thinking on how fast my baby is growing up."

"Mom, please don't start the gushy talk." Lindsey set her soda can on the table. "I'm too old for that."

"Never." She'd always be my baby.

"Yoo hoo!" Mom shoved against the screen door, loaded down with a pitcher and a platter.

"Cake!" Lindsey immediately perked up, losing the bored look teenagers loved to wear.

Duane jumped up to help her. "Do I get a piece of this before you women run me off?"

"I'll cut you a big slab right now, and you can run over to the house and share it with Leroy. He's watching some sports thing on TV."

Mom set the cake in the middle of the kitchen table and cut him a piece before transferring it to a paper plate. "There's hot coffee at the house, too. Now, git so we can go over our notes."

Duane froze. "Y'all are meeting about the killings?" He turned to me. "Didn't almost getting shot teach you anything?"

"Yes." I lifted my chin. "It taught me that I need to find out who is behind this before one of my family, or myself, end up dead."

He sighed. "Fine. Do what you want." Gripping the paper plate hard enough to bend it, he stormed out the front door.

My heart ached at his attitude, but I was now past the point of no return in this latest mystery. Squaring my shoulders, I plopped into a kitchen chair. "Since I can't write with my injured hand, I need you to take the notes, Lindsey."

"Uhm. Huh." Lindsey scooted the paper and pen toward her. "Last time, I almost got ran off the road and thrown in jail. I'm not sure I want to get shot at, Mom."

"I'm not going to put you in danger." I leaned my elbows on the table and rested my head in my hands. "The whole purpose here is to prevent someone else from dying. I just want you to brainstorm."

"Okay. I can do that."

"Me, too," Mom added. "Although, I don't mind a little danger in my life. It keeps things exciting." She pulled out another chair and sat. "Who are our suspects?"

"Well, I'm thinking Frank Powell. The newspaper has to be selling more copies since the deaths and the early obits. That gives him motive."

Lindsey made a suspect column and jotted down Frank's name.

"Put down Danny." Mom poured a cup of coffee and slid it to me. "Something about that boy seems a little off."

More than a little, in my opinion. His mom, too. "What about some of the ladies in the quilting circle? Would any of them have motives?"

Mom shrugged. "Not sure on that one. The victims are all older women living alone. That makes up the entire circle. Why would one of them want to kill one of their own?"

Good point. I drummed my fingernails on the table. There had to be something we were missing. Frank and Danny were too obvious, but both did warrant a closer investigation. Maybe I could slip some casual questions into our meeting on Friday. "Add Stacy to the suspect list. She'd do almost anything for a good story that would take her out of River Valley."

"You're just saying that because you don't like her," Mom stated, cutting into the cake.

"No, that's only a small part of it. I don't trust her. Never have. I'm also going to be asking some questions of your friends at the next quilting meeting."

Mom's hand stilled. "Do you really think one of them old women tried to shoot you?"

"Anything is possible. They all grew up in a time where everybody owned a gun. I bet most of them still do."

14

I flipped the store sign to open and unlocked the door. Five days after the glass shattering in my hand, I was able to remove the bandages and have more of my mobility. With it being Thursday, and the day for the quilters to come in and inspect their new room, I didn't want a glaring reminder of my gun ordeal. I'd rather have my questions catch them by surprise.

Bruce pulled his squad car in front of the coffee shop across the street, and I glanced at the clock. I should have left the house early enough to stop before coming to work. Where was Mom? The moment she showed, I would dash across the street for my morning java and maybe glean some information out of our overworked officer of the law.

There she was! Before she could enter, I dashed out. "Be back in a few." I raced across the street and barged into the coffee shop where I ran smack into Bruce's back.

He bent over at the waist, flailed his arms, and lost the battle with gravity. He hit the floor, taking a chair down with him.

"I'm so sorry." I rubbed my smashed nose with one hand and offered him the other.

"You're a menace." He grabbed my hand.

Out of my concern for him, I'd offered him my healing one. I yelped and released my hold, sending him back to the floor on his rear. "Sorry. Bad hand." I offered my other one.

"You wiped your nose with that one." He pushed to his feet.

"No, I didn't. I rubbed it." My eyes still smarted from the bump to the nose and the crush of my hand.

"I don't need your help, Marsha." He marched to the counter, keeping his gaze straight ahead.

Thankfully, few of the tables in the joint were filled, but there were enough to have witnessed our interaction. Chuckles bounced from table to table. Oh, well, I was used to embarrassing myself, but if the redness on the back of Bruce's neck was any indication, he wasn't.

I sidled up next to him and leaned against the counter while he ordered. "Any news on the case?"

"What case?"

I lowered my voice. "The one where we're trying to keep Dottie safe."

"You know I can't share information with you."

"But I'm part of this investigation!"

He narrowed his eyes. "How so?"

"Someone shot at me and threatened me."

"And you listened to them really well." He forked over the money for his cup of coffee. "I have someone patrolling in front of your house and Dottie's. That's all I can do without a suspect. Try to stay out of trouble. Duane really should put a leash on you." With a nod toward the barista, Bruce left the shop.

Whatever. I ordered my coffee and headed back to the shop just as the first of the quilters were arriving.

I greeted them all with a grin, a couple of them looking at me like I'd lost my mind, and tried to figure out exactly how I could grill them for information. I could tell from Mom's serious look that she concentrated on the same thing.

After Lindsey's reluctance to venture into anything remotely dangerous, which made me happy as her mother, Mom and I decided to cut the team down to two, with the occasional unwanted help from our men. Unless I was hurt or scared, then I definitely wanted Duane.

I pushed off from where I leaned against the door jamb and went to fetch the pitcher of iced tea. Still having no idea how to subtly ask questions, I filled another tray with finger sandwiches and homemade lemon squares. Maybe I could knock them off guard with treats.

Desserts served, I grabbed a doily I was crocheting and pulled up a chair. If I had to be in the room, I might as well get some work done.

Dottie glared at me. "The store owner isn't invited to join in, only to make sure our needs are met."

Witch. I almost wanted to blow her up myself.

"That's rude," Betty Larson, the leader, said. "Anyone is invited to pull up a chair." She gave me a smile. "I think Dottie must be off her fiber this morning, bless her heart."

I chuckled. No one can cut a person down more sweetly than an old southern woman.

"That's good." Mom started pouring tea. "We built this nice room for you ladies, and I would've hated going all Chuck Norris on you."

"You couldn't karate chop a baby bird if it was stuck in a trap." Dottie tossed some quilt squares on the table.

"We could step outside and I'll show you," Mom sputtered.

"Children." I took the pitcher away from Mom before she spilt something and ruined someone's quilt. "Let's work on our sewing and try to get along." Really. How old were these women, anyway? I felt like I was supervising a bunch of elementary students on the playground.

"So...anyone heard anything more about whether or not Nina's death was an accident?" I scanned the room, studying each woman's reaction.

Dottie rolled her eyes, Betty's mouth fell open and the other women, three in all, looked at each other with wide eyes. Three sisters, I didn't know the Bates women very well, just that they lived together, dressed the same, and were all born within ten to twelve months of each other. Maybe it wouldn't hurt to cozy up to them. They probably didn't miss much that went on in River Valley.

"Where are the other two women in the circle?" Weren't there two more last week?

"Well, Nancy is taking care of her grandson, Timmy," Betty explained. "He's the school's mascot. Seems he got into a bit of trouble. Started a fire behind the nursing home and is now on house arrest. How she can care for him, I'll never know. The boy is a bad seed.

"Why," she set her sewing in her lap. "I heard him tell her the other day that old people should be forced into nursing homes and put to sleep. Imagine." She shook her head. "Now, I realize he's most likely just upset about his consequences, but still…that statement was uncalled for."

"I'm sure he didn't mean that," Mom said. "Teenagers say lots of things they don't mean."

"Well, they found all kinds of chemistry sets and stuff in his room. I say he killed Nina and Mae." Betty jabbed her needle through her quilt.

My fingers itched for my notebook. Hopefully, between me and Mom, we'd remember everything the ladies said during their time together.

"That's ridiculous!" Dottie shook her head. "Everyone knows Stacy Tate is trying to get out of this town. She'll do anything for a big story." She waved a lemon square, dusting everyone with powdered sugar. "A teen boy wouldn't know how to rig a house to explode. Use your heads."

"You can find out anything on the internet." Betty took a sharp breath through her nose.

Okay, so far we had the snake mascot as a new suspect. No one seemed inclined to mention Frank and how the paper was failing. I tied off my thread and grabbed another color for the border. Since I now worked for the paper, I didn't think it ethical to mention him as a suspect.

"Sisters?" Addie Bates, the oldest of the three, glanced to one side then the other. "What do y'all think? Who in this town is capable of murdering old ladies? It's obvious Marsha needs our help."

Not exactly. Especially since moments ago, I'd wondered whether one of them could be a killer. I met Mom's glance, and shrugged. Might as well play along.

"It's true that we don't miss much," April, the youngest stated.

"Folks tend to overlook us," Alice, the middle one, added. "That's what comes of being respectful and minding our own business."

"Are you saying we should stay out of it?" Addie's eyes widened.

"Not at all. It sounds like great fun." Alice smiled and folded her hands on the table. "In the Agatha Christie mysteries, it's always the least likely suspect. Who do we suspect the least?"

I giggled. "My mother."

"That is not funny." Mom grabbed a cookie. "I am not a murderer."

"Says some," Dottie added. "You're at the top of my list."

"Who would benefit the most from Nina and Mae's death, then from stating Dottie is next?" Why couldn't Mom and Dottie stay on track?

"Dottie's next?" The three sisters all clutched their throats. "When?"

"We're down to two weeks now." I stared at Mom and warned her with my glare to keep her mouth shut. "But Dottie isn't taking the warning seriously."

"Why not?" The sisters leaned forward to get a better look at our next victim.

"Because it's silly, that's why." Dottie crossed her arms. "Putting someone's name in the paper thirty days before they die? Creative, but a waste of time, in my opinion. Why not just shoot the person in the head and get it over with? Besides, worrying won't make it less threatening. Only God knows my time."

"Blowing up someone's house while they're in it is less personal," April stated. "That way, the perp doesn't have to see his victim when they die. They keep themselves removed from the equation."

The ladies impressed me. Obviously, they gleaned a lot from mystery books.

"What we need to look for is motive," she continued. "People don't kill other people willy-nilly. Even gang initiations are for a reason."

Mom spewed her tea all over Dottie's quilt squares.

Dottie growled and pulled them closer to her. "If I'd wanted them antique looking, I would've soaked them in tea myself!"

"Sorry." Mom grabbed a rag and dabbed at the spill.

Maybe I wouldn't invite those two to the next sleuthing meeting, although their feud kept things interesting. I grinned. In addition to making a bit of money for the store, had the quilting circle also become an opportunity to solve a mystery? Had my gumshoe group gone from two to seven?

"Oh!" Dottie pointed a finger in the air. "There's that man who flipped me the bird at the diner the other day. I bet he's the killer. He had shifty eyes."

"Had you ever seen him before?" Betty asked. "Because, it's hard to believe a complete stranger from out of town would kill not one but two of our women."

"Maybe not, but he did yell out that elderly drivers should be euthanized. Maybe he's related to the school's mascot."

We all stared at Dottie like she'd sprouted horns. If I'd learned anything from the last mystery, it was that the culprit was usually someone we knew, which took us back to a motive. I could tell from the look on the Bates sisters' faces, that they were thinking something similar. Or maybe they were off in their only Bates world. No telling really.

Sighing, I put my doily back in the basket beside me and stood. There had to be paper and a pencil somewhere. If I had a willing group of people ready to help me, I wanted to take notes.

Finally. I grabbed a small spiral notebook from under the counter and the pencil stub next to it just as the bell over the front door jingled. I looked up to see Stacy, Darla, and Amber barge in, all three trying to crowd through the door at the same time.

While the picture was humorous, the three spelled trouble. I glanced over my shoulder at the work room. Why hadn't we insisted Leroy build a door? I was as sure as the sky was blue that all the women back there were straining their ears to hear who'd come in.

"Where is my son?" Darla demanded.

"Well, I don't know, maybe—"

Stacy planted her hands flat on the counter. "Don't tell this witch anything! She's out to hurt my sister."

Hmmm. "Amber's your sister?" I glanced from the meticulously made up Stacy to the Goth Amber. Never would have guessed that one.

15

"You're sister is a wanton girl who seduced my boy." Darla's face reddened. She poked Stacy's chest with her forefinger so sharp, I almost feared she'd pop the silicone inside.

"It takes two to tango, missy." Stacy put her arm around Amber.

I glanced over my shoulder. Yep, the quilting ladies all stared around the corner, not trying in the least to be subtle. "Would you three like to take this somewhere private?"

"Nothing's going to be private for long." A drop of spittle hung on Darla's bottom lip. "Everyone in town will know within two months."

Oh. Danny was going to be a daddy. Well, goodness. "It isn't the end of the world, Darla. Young people jump into things all the time."

She spun on me like a cat after a catnip-filled toy. "What would you know? You aren't alone to raise that daughter of yours. You have your mother. It's been just me and Danny since the day he was born. My mother was nothing but a drug user and died alone in her apartment. No one discovered her body for a week. A week! So, keep your opinions to yourself."

How horrible. Darla might be a prickly woman with the personality of a skunk, but my heart felt for her. I understood a bit more why she never seemed happy at her job at the newspaper. She probably never felt happy ever.

"I'm sorry to tell you, but Danny isn't here. If he's working with Leroy today, they're probably over at the house working on a new porch." I plastered what I hoped was a sympathetic smile on my face. "Looks like he'll need the money more than ever now."

"Don't simper at me." Darla spun on her heel. "We'll have nothing to do with the brat."

Amber burst into tears and buried her face into Stacy's blown up chest. My smile faded as fast as a falling rock. It was hard to be sympathetic to a woman who oozed discontent, no matter how hard a person tried.

"Come on, Amber." Stacy guided her sister toward the door. "I'll take care of you. We don't need them."

"But Danny loves me. He said he did. It's that evil woman who's behind this." Amber raised her head. Mascara and black eyeliner ran down her cheeks in dark rivers.

"And Danny is too spineless to stand up to his mother. We all know that." Stacy ushered her outside.

Well, it had been an interesting morning so far, and I couldn't write any of it in the gossip column for tomorrow's edition. I grinned. Of course, it wouldn't hurt to mention Darla would be a grandmother. Maybe making it public knowledge would force her to take some measure of responsibility or force her no-good son to man up. I could also be opening a huge can of worms, considering Darla knows I write the column.

*

The next morning, having dug up a few more tidbits while eating at Wanda's Diner the night before, I slid the folder across the conference table to Frank. I also managed to sell a couple of ads at the last minute, by practically begging friends of Mom's who owned their own businesses. Because of this, Frank sat grinning like a fool.

Which was almost as scary looking as his scowl. Instead of his eyes disappearing under a hanging brow, they now disappeared behind wrinkled cheeks covered by a big-toothed grin that reminded me a bit of a shark.

He tapped the folder on the table and glanced at Stacy. "Well, what have you got? Any good stories?"

"No, sir." Stacy slumped in her chair. "Family problems interfered."

Frank's grin turned to a frown. "That's unacceptable. With the problems this paper is having, we can't afford to have sloppy work. I want a newsworthy story in my email before midnight tonight so we can squeak it into this weekend's edition."

"What do you want me to write about?"

He slammed his fist on the table. "I don't know! You're the reporter. Must I go out and drum up stories myself! I have before, and can again. But that's what I pay you for."

Feeling sorry for her berating, I almost offered her the story of getting shot at, but considering that happened a few days ago, it was hardly newsworthy anymore. I searched my mind for something else...and came up empty. There wasn't much that went on in River Valley. Oh!

"Why don't you write about the names that are appearing in the obituaries thirty days before the person dies of suspicious circumstances?" There. The answer to her problem and, quite possibly, a more legal upfront way of me finding out information.

"What's this?" Frank asked. "People are dying?"

"Technically, people die every day, Frank." I fought not to roll my eyes. "But in this instance, people's names are showing up *before* they die."

"Why hasn't anyone told me?" He glanced from me to Stacy.

"Hasn't Officer Barnett questioned you?" Darn that Bruce. He told me he would investigate.

"No one has said anything to me." Stacy studied her manicured nails. "It might make an interesting story. Especially if I'm the one who solves the mystery." The sliver of a smile flickered on her lips. "Reporter goes after story, finds herself in danger, and solves the murders. Of course, I won't really put myself in danger. That would be elaboration for the paper."

I narrowed my yes. Did Stacy confirm my suspicions that someone was killing people they thought would be expendable in order to sell more papers? "Are any of us in danger of losing our jobs if the paper does poorly?"

"Of course we are." Frank shook his head. "You need to sell more ads, and Stacy needs to write better news breaking stories. If the paper folds, it won't be just one of us out on the streets, it'll be the whole staff." He grabbed the folders in front of him and stood. "So, get your rear ends out there and do your jobs."

Of course, Country Gifts from Heaven was my main job. The newspaper was for extra cash, and the opportunity to snoop under cover of working on the paper. I'd gotten myself in a jam. Country Gifts provided my living, but a good work ethic wouldn't allow me to do a shoddy job on the paper. Now, the lack of time to effectively do both jobs teased me.

"Go!" Frank banged both hands on the table top, sending Stacy and me to our feet and crashing into each other on our way through the door.

"So, Stacy," I said once we were in the hall. "I didn't know you and Amber were sisters." I smoothed the skirt of the dress I wore. "I love the boutique she works at."

"The one my mother owns?" Stacy turned and glared. "Well, stepmother. Amber and I are half-sisters." She stopped. "Why am I telling you this? It's none of your business what kind of drama goes on in my family."

"True, but I've always been told I have a very sympathetic ear."

"Whatever." Her heels tapped out an angry rhythm as she marched away. "My stepmother is nothing but a worthless old hag who belongs in a nursing home. Making Amber take care of her after her stroke. It's inhumane—" She clamped her lips closed and continued on her way.

Well, alrighty then. That raised a bunch of new questions. Ones I hoped Mom could answer.

Oh, no! Catching a glimpse of a calendar hanging in someone's cubicle, I fished my cell phone out of my cavernous purse. "Mom? Do you know what tomorrow is?"

"Of course I do. It's Lindsey's sixteenth birthday party."

"I'm going to be a little late coming in this morning. I still haven't ordered her cake, or purchased decorations. Please tell me invitations went out."

"Over a week ago. What in the world would you do without me?"

I continued my way to the lobby. "I'd be a total failure." Once this mystery was solved, I could get back to my own version of an organized life. Which wasn't very organized, but it was all I had. That and my aspirations to do better.

When I stopped in front of Darla's desk, she turned her computer screen away from me and cupped the mouth piece of the phone. "I don't care what you want. I'm the boss here, and I say she has to go!"

Interesting. I stepped closer to her desk, now looking for something, anything, in my purse. My hand curled around a tube of lipstick that had to be from the 90s. When was the last time I wore anything other than a clear gloss?

"I'm not sure you realize who you're talking to." Her voice hissed, sending a shiver down my spine. I got the impression Darla was not a woman to get on the bad side of. "You said you would go with me tomorrow... I don't care if I wasn't invited...You can't go back on your word. We'll discuss this later. Marsha, may I help you?"

I'd been so engrossed in looking busy, I hadn't realized when she'd hung up the phone. "There it is!" I held up the lipstick, ignored the gunk gathered around the lid, and pulled the top off to smear the ruby red color across my lips. If I'd paid closer attention before actually acting as if I wanted to wear lipstick, I would've realized it was left over from a prior Halloween.

"That isn't really your color." Darla crossed her arms. "And you have lint stuck on your bottom lip. It looks like you've been kissing someone's belly button."

Heavens! I picked at the fuzzy stuff on my lip and tried to come up with a reason for stopping by her desk.

Darla sighed. "Well? Did you want something, or were you eavesdropping on my phone conversation?"

Boy, she was good. If she wasn't on my list of possible suspects, I'd enlist her help. "Uh, do you have any possible leads for advertising? Frank's on my case about the paper needing money, and well..."

"You want me to do your job, in other words."

"No, but you've been here longer, and might know the type of businesses that would pay for advertising."

"Any business that wants to increase their profits will want to advertise." Darla turned back to her computer. "All you have to do is pound the pavements and ask. Some will say yes, some will say no."

"Thanks." I guessed. Tossing the old tube of lipstick into a nearby trashcan, I headed into the mid-morning sun and glanced up and down the street.

River Valley was not a metropolitan city. Main Street consisted of maybe twenty businesses, ten on each side of the street, with one street branching off to form a plus sign. That side road had maybe four shops. Thankfully, one of them sold party goods. Then, a quick run by the grocery store and I'd have the important elements of Lindsey's party—oh, my gosh, we'd need food.

Sub sandwiches would do. I high-tailed it to the party store and made a beeline to the party lights and teen section, most of which was, thankfully, hot pink with some black thrown in. I was pretty sure no one would want me to come up with a color scheme on my own, and Lindsey loved pink and black. Arms loaded down with lights, streamers and all the paper dishes I could carry, I rushed toward the counter.

"I will kill you." A voice drifted from the aisle behind me. "If you touch her, say anything to her, I will cut you so deep, you'll cry for your mother."

I whirled and knocked over a stack of stuffed animals. Somehow keeping my grip on my things, I thrust them into the cashier's arms, "I'll be back," then dashed out the door.

All I needed was for someone threatening murder to catch me eavesdropping.

16

I was pretty positive the voice I heard was Stacy's. Who in the world could she be threatening so cold-heartedly?

Leaning against the concrete block walls of the building, I tried to ignore the fact I stood in a dirty alley and focused on my breathing. The purchases on the counter needed paid for and taken home, regardless of an overheard phone conversation that sent spiders dancing up and down my spine.

After taking a couple of deep breaths, I moseyed back into the store and approached the counter. "Do you have my order ready? The one I placed earlier this morning?"

The girl looked at me as if my eyes had turned yellow. "This stuff?"

"Yes, of course. Thank you so much for having it ready. How much do I owe you?"

"I'll ... have to ring it up." She shook her head and glanced over my shoulder, shrugging.

I followed her gaze. Stacy glared from the section of baby shower items.

"Are you following me?" she asked.

"No, I'm picking up decorations for my daughter's party tomorrow. Are you planning a baby shower?" Amber didn't show yet in her pregnancy, but some people were known to start things early.

"I'm just browsing." She looked as if she wanted to say something else, but instead, turned and rushed out the door.

"This has been the strangest morning," the cashier said. "You throw things at me, she yells at someone on the phone, and some guy comes in to buy balloons, starts to cry, and doesn't buy anything."

"I didn't mean to toss my purchases at you." There was no explanation that wouldn't make me sound like a Looney Tune, so I left it at that. After leaving her a card with the newspaper's advertising information on it for her to give to the owner, and with my purchases now in bags, I headed back down the sidewalk to my car.

If I'd planned ahead, I would have thought to drive down the street and save myself the back and forth walking. Although, the exercise has done me good. Between two jobs, limited time to dig into my M&Ms, and parking away from shopping, I'd managed to drop a few pounds.

The door to the dress boutique beckoned. When had I turned from overalls to dresses? Maybe a new dress for dinner that night. Duane actually had the night off from football practice and was taking me out to eat somewhere other than Wanda's

Diner. I stowed my bags in the trunk of my car and almost skipped to the boutique.

What? Locked? I cupped my hands around my eyes and peered through the glass.

Maybe the shop was closed because of pregnancy? In mourning because of Danny and his deadbeat mother. Oh, well. I had another dress I'd bought last week I could wear to dinner. After another glance through the window, I turned, then stopped.

When had the store started selling black combat boots? Those didn't fit the rest of the inventory at all, and I'd definitely spotted a pair tossed next to the counter. I fished my cell phone from my pocket and called 9-1-1.

Ten minutes later, Bruce runs down the street, one hand on the butt of his pistol. He stopped next to me and bent at the waist, panting for breath. "Should...have...known."

What? That I would be here? "I think Amber, the clerk in this store, is injured inside."

"What makes...you think so?" Bruce straightened, hands on his hips.

"They don't sell combat boots here, and there is a pair next to the counter. Plus, the store is closed in the middle of the day. Don't you think that's odd?"

"I think you need to pray to the Almighty God to cure you of your affliction."

"What affliction?"

"The one that compels you to stick your nose where it doesn't belong." Bruce tapped on the locked door, then peered inside.

"See the boots?"

"Yep, and I see the striped sock that goes in them, too. I think." He took the club off his belt and bashed in the door. "Stay back."

I'd stay back while glass rained down, but I'd follow him so closely in the store, we'd share the same perfume. We rushed around the counter. The shoes were empty. The striped socks was actually a scarf draped over the heel of one of the shoes.

"That's weird."

Bruce shook his head. "I should've known nothing was up the moment I found out it was you that called."

"Oh, stop it. It's still strange that the door is locked in the middle of the day."

"Whatever." He continued through a door behind the counter and down a short hall.

I followed, peering into a closet and small restroom. Regardless of Bruce's opinion, something was not right. I pushed open the door to the alley.

Amber and Danny jumped apart like two scalded cats. From the smear of scarlet lipstick on Danny's mouth, they weren't whispering secrets. I crossed my arms and grinned at sneaky young love. Stacy would have a heart attack.

"This is why the store is locked?" High spots of color glowed on Bruce's cheeks. "Your mother would have a fit if she knew. Once she recovers from her stroke, she's going to be coming back to work and doesn't need to pull this place back up from the dumps." With a curt nod, he marched away.

Amber's eyes filled with tears, and she two-hand shoved Danny away from her. "I told you this was not a good idea."

"We're just kissing." He followed her into the store.

Well, it had been a long time, but if I remembered correctly, kissing is what started everything that resulted in me having Lindsey. Mystery of the locked store solved, I strolled back to my car and drove to the grocery store to order Lindsey's cake and giant sub. Mom was probably having a fit by now, wondering what was taking me so long.

I checked my cell phone. Nope, no messages. I sent Mom a quick text telling her I was still shopping, then pulled out of town and headed down the highway. The small store in River Valley wouldn't have the type of cakes suitable for a sweet sixteen, and I wanted my baby's day to be as special as I could make it.

"Wow." Duane stepped through the front door. "You look amazing. What's up with the change?"

"You've noticed?" I smoothed the skirt of my dress.

"That you've been dressing in something other than overalls and getting thinner?" He put his hands on my waist and pulled me close. "You bet I have. I like it. I didn't think it possible for you to get any better." He nuzzled my neck, making my knees weak. I giggled.

"I thought we were going out to dinner." I planted my palms on his chest. The feel of his sculpted muscles did things to me that should be unlawful. "If you keep kissing me, we'll never leave."

"Promises, promises." He planted another lingering one on my lips, then stepped back. "Hurry up and set a wedding date, would you? I'm dying over here."

That made two of us. Blood simmering like a pot over a low fire, I stepped into the early evening air and made my way to Duane's truck. Heels, even low kitten ones, made walking on gravel tricky. Maybe I should've practiced.

Duane took my arm to steady me and helped me into his truck. "Maybe you should wear sneakers to the wedding."

"Ha ha." I smoothed my dress and clicked the seatbelt into place. I'd already planned on wearing flip-flops. Bejeweled ones, of course.

We spoke of love, the someday wedding, and other routine things until we sat down at the table and ordered our steaks. I glanced around the restaurant, approving of the muted lighting and scattered tables which provided a little privacy. Very romantic.

"So, I heard you didn't show up for work today?" Duane reached across the table and took my hand.

"Mom has a big mouth. I had a meeting at the paper, then went shopping for Lindsey's party tomorrow." Which, thankfully, I'd finished. I filled him in on the rest of the day's strange proceedings.

"Hmmm." He straightened and reached for his glass of ice water. "That doesn't look good for

Stacy, does it? But then again, people threaten to kill people all the time."

"Yeah, but most of them don't mean it." I stared at the flicker of the candle in the center of the table. Dad always said he hated dim restaurants. Couldn't see where to put the food in order to eat. "I think she was talking to Danny."

"And then he rushed right over to the shop to smooch on his girl. Brave boy." Duane straightened as the waitress brought us our food.

"Or stupid." We bowed our heads while Duane said the blessing, then I cut into my steak, forking a piece to my mouth. Yum. Crusty blue-cheese on top of a perfectly cooked filet. Pure heaven. "I have to admit, though, that I haven't a clue as to who is killing off these old ladies. I'm really worried about Dottie. Time is running out."

"Have you stopped to pray about it?" Duane patted my hand. "No offense, sweetheart, but everyone knows how you tend to take the reins and gallop off without guidance."

"True, and no, I haven't taken the proper time to pray." Remorse spread through my stomach. Why didn't I pray first and act second? I knew the proper way to approach any situation, yet I constantly forgot. God must spend a lot of time shaking His head at me.

"Once you do, things will start falling into place." Duane winked. "Just remember, you promised not to go investigating alone."

"I won't." I wasn't sure if he would be relieved to know I didn't go anywhere without my pistol or my Tazer. That might raise a bunch of new worries.

It still boggled my mind that such a handsome, got-my-life-together, man wanted to marry me.

I glanced out the window into the gathering dusk. Stacy stood next to a pillar on the patio, phone to her ear, arms waving with punctuation to her conversation. Why did that woman show up everywhere I went?

"Don't even think about it." Duane set his fork and knife on the edge of his plate.

"What?"

"It's killing you not to rush out there and find out what has her so upset."

"Yes, but that doesn't mean I will." I reached for my iced tea. Seriously. People were always thinking the worst of me. You'd think I had no sense of my own.

"She's dealing with a lot right now." He leaned on the table. "Since her mother suffered that stroke, Stacy is struggling to work her own job, keep the store going, and watch out for her younger sister. That's a lot for one woman to have to do alone."

"I did it alone for years, Duane." From the moment my husband died to Duane's return, I'd been a single mother. Sure, I had my mom's help, but I could sympathize with Stacy.

"Not everyone is as strong as you." He crossed his arms and leaned back in the booth.

"Maybe not, but everyone appreciates a little help now and again."

He sighed. "Are we arguing over the fact I left town and didn't return until a few months ago?"

"I don't know. Are we?" I raised my eyebrows.

"Is that why you've held off setting a wedding date? Because you're afraid I'll leave again?" His face fell. "I love you, Marsha. Someday, you'll accept the fact you can be loved for the wonderful person that you are, and you'll accept the gift. For now, I'll wait."

My insecurities wanted me to ask if he'd wait forever if that's what it took, but that wouldn't be fair to him. "I'm sorry. I really don't know what's gotten into—"

Duane reached across the table, dragged me across the polished surface, scattering dishes to the floor as he dove

17

Duane half-carried, half-dragged me toward the kitchen as a green sedan crashed through the window behind where I'd sat. Glass rained on the table and onto the floor, crunching under my feet. Screams rent the air. The car's alarm blared.

"Are you okay?" Once behind the swinging doors of the kitchen, Duane turned and cupped my face. "You aren't cut anywhere?"

I shook my head. "No, a few bruises maybe, but I'm fine." I stood on tip-toe and peered out the glass circle in the door. "We should go see if anyone needs any help."

"Stay close." Duane took my hand, and we re-entered chaos.

What poor fool had lost control of their car? I pulled free of Duane's grip and rushed toward the car, him close on my heels.

No one sat slumped behind the wheel. I searched the floor and surrounding area. Had they walked away? Been moved by someone? "There's no one here." Without touching the car, I peered through the window. "Duane, come look."

An elastic cord stretched from the steering wheel to somewhere under the seat. A rebar was propped on the gas pedal and wedged against the seat. Pretty old school, but effective. "Someone ran the car through the window on purpose." And right toward the table where Duane and I were eating.

Somebody meant to run over me. Since I'd still been checking obituaries regularly, and hadn't spotted my name, I must have been closer to solving the mystery than I thought. If his pale face was any indication, Duane obviously had the same thought.

He knelt to help a woman cut by flying glass, the muscle in his jaw ticking. Poor man. First, we almost get into an argument, then we're almost killed, and then we were surrounded by people with minor bleeding wounds. I moved to help, and stopped.

Duane was almost killed.

Someone was after me.

The man I loved had also become a target.

I sagged against a table. How could I get out of trying to find the killer? If doing so put Duane in danger, I wanted nothing more to do with any of it. Not even if it meant Dottie might be harmed. She was Bruce's responsibility. Duane was mine. For the first time I could remember, I contemplated quitting something.

"What's wrong?" Duane righted a chair and helped me into it. "You look really pale."

"I need to find a way out of this." Panic rose in my throat, threatening to choke me. To take away my breath and cloud my mind. Of course I was pale. We'd almost been squashed by a runaway vehicle. "You're in danger. My family is at risk." I gripped his shirt. My breath caught. "How do I get out?"

"Settle down." He crouched beside me, taking my hands in his. "You can't. Not from the moment someone shot at you." He exhaled slowly, the sound as sad as the escape of someone's hope. "All we can do is try and stay safe until the culprit is caught."

I shook my head hard enough to send my hair flying around my face. "It's impossible. Someone I love is going to be hurt." His face swam in front of me, followed by Lindsey's and Mom's. A sob rose in my chest, constricting my breathing. Not usually prone to anxiety attacks, I couldn't breathe, which only served to increase my panic.

Duane noticed my distress. "Did someone call 9-1-1?"

"I did," an older woman said.

"Me, too." A teenager squatted next to a man in black slacks, the sleeve of the man's arm stained with blood.

The room looked as if a bomb had gone off. My chest tightened, and my vision grew blurry. What was wrong with me? I slumped forward.

When I woke, I was lying on a stretcher in the middle of the parking lot with an oxygen mask over my face and Bruce frowning down at me. Not a sight I thought I'd ever wake up to. I pulled the mask away from my face. "What do you want?"

"Oh, good, you're alive." He pulled out his notebook. "So, someone tried to kill you?"

"Who told you that?" I struggled to a sitting position. My head spun.

"Duane said you said something to that affect then passed out. The paramedic said you most likely had an anxiety attack, and they'd take care of you after they patch up the bleeding folks. So, here we are again, me asking you questions because someone no longer wants you around."

"There are others who aren't going to be around much longer if you don't start doing your job."

"We're short staffed, Marsha. I'm doing the best I can. No one has forgotten about the threat against Dottie."

My shoulders slumped. "You're right. I'm sorry." I had no choice but to see this thing through. Lives depended on me.

"Mom?" Lindsey barreled through the onlookers and threw herself at me. Behind her, rushed Mom and Leroy.

"Bruce called us," Mom explained. "Are you all right?"

"I'm fine." I tightened my arms around my daughter and held on for dear life. What if I'd never seen her beautiful face again? Witnessed that teenage roll of her eyes whenever I annoyed her?

Mom petted my head. "We have to stop this. People were only injured today, but they could've been killed. This parking lot looks like something out of a nightmare."

"All because someone wants me to stop investigating."

"They won't stop now." Mom shook her head. "There's too much at stake. They'll still go after Dottie. They'll most likely keep coming after you, so we'll keep searching. How do we get mixed up in these things?"

"There is no 'we', Mom." I struggled to my feet. "I'm doing this alone now." I glared at Bruce, daring him to contradict me.

He closed his eyes and shook his head. "I never thought I'd say this, but I need all the help I can get. Even if the only help available is a nosey woman." Still shaking his head, he meandered off to interview someone else. I could've sworn a pig flew across the sky at that moment.

"Oh, no, you don't." Mom planted fists on her hips. "We're in this together. Except for Lindsey. We don't want to risk her. She's young and still has her whole life ahead of her."

There went the eye roll from my daughter I loved so well. I held out my hand. "Help me up, kid."

Lindsey grabbed my hand and yanked. "Anyone want ice cream?"

"Me, just as soon as the paramedics are convinced it's safe for me to get out of here." I spotted Duane by the ambulance and waved.

He trotted to my side. "Ready? They said you could go home."

"We're going out for ice cream." I put my arm around Lindsey's shoulders. "To celebrate life. You want to come?"

"Wouldn't miss it." He slipped an arm around my waist. "We all have some plans to make."

Oh, I liked the sound of that, maybe. Wait. What if the plans were for Duane to become more involved in finding the murderer? No, I couldn't sit back and let him put himself in more danger. I'd stop him somehow.

Lindsey rode with Duane and me to the local ice cream parlor. My body ached from Duane's tackle, and it would sport a variety of colored bruises tomorrow, but if my daughter wanted an ice cream with me, then that's what she'd get. Time spent together became more rare the older she got.

We all managed to squeeze into a large booth at the ice cream parlor, me squashed between Duane and Lindsey. After asking what everyone wanted, Duane left to fill our orders.

"Were you scared?" Lindsey peered sideways at me.

"I didn't know what was happening until Duane yanked me across the table. Thank God, he saw the car coming." If he hadn't, we'd both be in the morgue and my precious daughter would be staring at my lifeless body.

"Playing football gave that boy fast reflexes." Mom tapped a straw on the table. "We could use him on our sleuthing team."

"I don't want anyone else involved." I squared my shoulders. "Someone is after me. If one of y'all get hurt or killed because of a choice I made, I'll never be able to live with myself."

"Don't be ridiculous." Mom drew air through her nose loud enough for me to hear. "I'm your mother. If I want to help you, I will. Same goes for your future husband." She patted Leroy's shoulder.

"Not even a loving husband can keep a momma bear away from her cub. Leroy won't say a word to stop me."

He opened his mouth to say something, then closed it and shrugged instead.

I smiled, her words warming my heart. "We're not arguing about this. Now, anyone have any idea whose car went through the steak house window?"

"Not a clue," Leroy said. "But, I'll be asking around tomorrow. My guess is that the car was stolen. Somebody is pretty smart in these parts. Takes some skill to blow up houses and rig up a car the way that one was."

"Oh, pooh." Mom smacked his shoulder. "You can learn anything on the internet. Everyone knows that."

"Maybe so, but I still don't think we're working with a dummy."

I agreed with Leroy. We weren't working with a dummy. Now, to find out the identity of that non-dummy.

"Any great crime solving discussed while I was gone?" Duane handed out chocolate-covered-peanut-caramel pieces of heaven on a stick.

"No." I bit into my treat, relishing the taste of frozen chocolate. "But I'll be keeping an eagle eye open at Lindsey's party tomorrow."

"Don't embarrass me, Mom."

So much for daughterly concern. "I promise I'll be subtle, sweetie."

"Yeah. Right."

I'm pretty sure if Duane didn't have her blocked in, she would have scooted out and deserted us. A few months ago, she'd gone sneaking past the very window I now looked out of while chasing a boy who happened to be a primary thief suspect. Instead, he'd turned out to be a nice boy, one she got tired of rather quickly and dumped. Or maybe Bobby dumped her. Either way, their relationship didn't last long.

Not only had she gone chasing after the boy, but she'd caught me in a compromising position with Duane after we attempted to chase her down. Oh, the delights of being a mother in love with a teenage daughter who I constantly kept on the verge of ridicule from her friends.

"How many of your classmates are coming tomorrow?" I asked.

"Pretty much all of the Sophomore class."

"Oh. How many exactly is that?"

"About ninety."

I needed to buy a bigger cake. The ice cream sat like a cold stone in my stomach. And we'd need a few more sub sandwiches.

Lindsey giggled. "Just kidding. I didn't invite everyone. Only about eighty."

Oh, well, that was so much better. Eighty teenagers and assorted adults meant the party would have to be moved outside. Good thing we'd had good weather so far.

Maybe Leroy and Duane could man a fire pit and we could add S'mores to the menu. I really should have bought invitations for her to hand out so we could've kept a better handle on the amount of people invited.

The only good thing I could come up with for that many people is the amount of information I might be able to gather. Surely with half the town in my backyard, somebody would have a clue what was happening in River Valley.

18

The lines were drawn.

High school kids goofed off around one fire pit, adults huddled around another, and the numbers were vastly uneven. With the amount of young people in attendance, Lindsey might as well have hung up a sign saying, "Party at my house." Half the school seemed to be there.

With twinkle lights strung on every tree and bush, tables laden with food and plastic crates full of iced soda, there wasn't much else the youngsters needed. Duane had even set up a badminton net at one end of the yard and some kids had a healthy competition going on.

I'd kept the door to the cottage open, with the bedroom doors locked. Easy access to the restroom and peace of mind for me.

I settled back in a lawn chair and prepared to enjoy a time of people-watching. Nothing was more fun than watching teenagers when they didn't know they were being watched. In a while, once the guests were comfortable and conversation flowed freely, I'd make the rounds and see what information I could dig up.

"Mom." Lindsey glared down at me. "Are you going to sit there all night?"

"I was planning on it. Why?"

"Someone needs to stand by the punch bowl. I've already dumped it out once, and since it's my party, I don't want to spend it supervising."

Uh-oh. "What's happening?"

"Someone keeps spiking the punch."

My daughter is the best thing since sliced bread. "Do we know who the culprit is?"

"If I knew that, I'd have Uncle Duane kick them out." She gave me one of those teenage looks signifying I was as bright as a box of rocks.

Sighing, I pushed out of my chair. "I'll watch the table. I'm very proud of you, sweetie."

"Don't embarrass me." She glanced around to make sure no one was watching, then hurried back over to a group of girls.

I shrugged and headed to my assigned position. Maybe supervising the snack table would allow me to snoop without attracting unwanted attention. I'd managed to garner quite a bit of info at Mom's and Leroy's engagement party a few months ago, while trying to solve the mystery of things disappearing, literally under their owners' noses. Of course, that party was mostly adults, but sometimes kids knew things they weren't aware they knew.

Once I reached the table set up on the side of the house, I sniffed the contents. Still suspicious, I poured a small glass, took a sip, and promptly spewed it into the bushes. Darn, those kids. Well, no more punch. If we'd already wasted two bowls full, I wasn't about to make any more. Sorry, Lindsey. The guests would have to be satisfied with water and soda.

The chip bowl was empty, so I reached under the table for a full bag. Straightening, I dumped the bag into the bowl just as Darla and the man who had flipped Dottie off in the diner parking lot strolled onto my lawn.

Over by the main house, Danny stood in the shadows talking to Amber. If Darla spotted him, fireworks would fill the sky. Just when I thought things couldn't get any more interesting, Stacy sauntered into view, hanging on the arm of some stud-muffin of a stranger. Lindsey giggled from something her ex-boyfriend, Bobby, whispered in her ear.

Was this a birthday party or a dating service?

"Hey, good looking." Duane snuck up and nuzzled my neck.

"Hey, yourself." I turned into his arms. "Is this not the strangest sweet sixteen party you've ever seen? It's more like a Valentine's Day party."

"Hmmm." He turned me to where my back was to him and rested his chin on the top of my head. "Most likely it's just people feeling good because it's one of the few nice weather days left before winter sets in."

"But where did they all come from? I'm sure Lindsey didn't invite Stacy or Darla. Danny, maybe, and Amber, but where did the adults get notice?"

"Word travels fast." His arms tightened, snuggling me closer. There was no better feeling in the world than having my beloved's arms around me. Pretty much the way it felt to have God's arms around me: Safe and loved. "People hear the word 'party' and show up in droves."

"If Darla sees Danny rubbing Amber's belly, we might have another murder on our hands." I reluctantly slid free of Duane's hold. "I'd best warn him to take his little cozy conversation somewhere else." What I'd really like to do was tell his mother to leave, but I was pretty certain Danny was the easier of the two to face.

Before I made it to his side, Dottie stopped me. "Okay, Marsha. Now that the day of my imminent death is drawing near, I must confess I'm getting a bit nervous. I'd like you to stay with me on the 30th and the 31st day."

My mouth opened and closed like a fish on land. As much as I didn't want anything to happen to the older woman, staying with her for two days would put me in the line of fire. I was pretty sure Duane wouldn't allow me to guard her.

"I see your reluctance, but I'm begging you." She took my hand, her skin soft and paper thin. "I'm pretty sure nothing will happen, but why chance it? The other women died alone. I live at the retirement home, but…my name did appear in the obits. I'll just tell the aides at the home that we're having a sleepover."

True, she did live in a place where she was constantly surrounded by people. What could possibly go wrong? "Okay, but only for those two nights."

"And days." She raised her eyebrows.

I sighed. "And days. You do realize I have a daughter, right?"

"Gertie will be more than happy to watch her for a couple of days."

True. Mom would like nothing more, and considering the danger to Dottie, I wouldn't recommend that Mom stay with her instead. I patted Dottie on the shoulder. "We'll talk more when the day gets closer."

A few very crude words shot across the lawn. I whirled as Stacy steamrolled toward Darla. Minus her usual daily suit, and not counting her enlarged top half, Stacy could've blended in with the teenagers in her skinny jeans and tight tee-shirt. Darla's date tried to step between them, but Darla shoved him to the side. Stacy slapped her across the face. Darla's head whipped to the side.

She screamed and lunged, grabbing Stacy's hair in both hands. Seconds later, the two women rolled on my autumn brown lawn like two wrestlers. Their shrieks were enough to pierce the heavens, their words heated enough to raise hell.

"Call Bruce." Duane rushed past me. He grabbed Darla around the waist and lifted her off the ground while Leroy did the same to Stacy.

I dug my cell phone out of the pocket of my jeans and called Bruce's personal number. "Hey, Bruce. We got a fight over here at Lindsey's party. Can you come take care of it?"

"Did you break them up? I don't know why you invited every kid in town to your house. That's a recipe for disaster."

"This fight is between two of the female adults. Duane and Leroy broke them up, but it looks like one of them might be bleeding."

"Wish I could have seen that. Be there in five minutes." Click.

Duane and Leroy forced their charges into lawn chairs and stood guard. Leroy thrust a handkerchief into Stacy's hands. She held it to her bleeding face.

Teenagers flocked to the scene like children after the candy, when a piñata got busted. Lindsey looked ready to cry. I'd reassure her later that the fight only made her party a huge success. Something her friends would talk about for weeks.

After glaring at the two immature women, I hurried to the front yard to wait for Bruce. Why hadn't Stacy's and Darla's escorts broke them up instead of standing there grinning like fools? What had the two women so at odds with each other? Surely it wasn't because their younger family members did the tango under the sheets and now have a baby on the way. Unfortunately, lots of teenagers make that mistake too early. There had to be something else at the root of their hatred for each other.

Darla was at least ten years older than Stacy, maybe more. Darla was divorced, Stacy never married. Darla was a newcomer to town, so the chances of Stacy having committed adultery with the other woman's husband seemed slim. I sat on the top porch step and rested my chin in my hands.

Stacy, Darla, Dottie, Danny…the names whirled in a circle in my head. What was I missing?

The first two victims joined the melee. Elderly women living alone. Danny lived with his grandparents. Did Darla live there, too?

No, she couldn't. Her mother was dead. Died alone in her apartment. Danny lived with his paternal grandparents. My head ached with all the questions. And…what did any of it have to do with the murders?

Bruce pulled into the drive, lights off, thank goodness, and halted my mind spinning. He stepped out of the car, sunglasses on despite it being nine p.m., and marched in my direction. "I don't hear any screaming."

"You will." I stood. "Follow me on back." Leading the way to where Duane and Leroy still held guard, I realized there were a lot of questions I needed to talk to Bruce about. After all, didn't he say he could use my help because of short-staffing? Maybe if I put my brain with his, we could actually find some answers.

"Thank God." Stacy stood and wagged the bloody handkerchief in Bruce's face. "This witch broke my nose. Do you know how much this nose cost me?"

"She hit me first." Darla leaped to her feet. "There're plenty of witnesses to attest to that fact."

"You're a liar!" Stacy whirled so fast, her hair stuck in a smear of blood above her lip. I grimaced and turned my head, although I did wish I had my camera.

"Ladies, please." Bruce pulled out his ever present notebook. "One at a time. Mrs. Quincy, you first." He peered over his sunglasses at Darla.

She took a deep breath and started talking faster than a home run baseball disappearing over the shortstop's head. "I was walking with my date…Roy Sims…and this harlot attacked me. Right out in front of God and everybody! Look at my face. I swear there are going to be permanent scars. Why, I ought to—"

"You defamed my little sister's character!" Stacy stepped so close, her bloody nose almost touched Darla's. "You and that no-account son of yours. Then, when she needs him the most, you want him to walk away without owning up to his responsibilities. What kind of mother does that?" She grinned. "Oh, yes, I know all about your mother, Darla. Oh yes, I do."

Darla shrieked and lunged, talons raised. "You leave her out of this!"

Bruce stepped between them, one hand on his Tazer. "Ladies, if you continue this, I'll have no choice but to take you down."

I would've loved seeing either one of them on the ground twitching like a worm. When I'd bought my Tazer, the irresistible arc of blue light beckoned my finger, and Duane found me on the porch flopping like a fish. It might be fun to see my nemesis in that predicament.

Darla called Stacy another name not fit for children's ears, one of the football players laughed, and then the mascot, Timmy Weldon, stepped out of my cottage with a can of lighter fluid in his hand.

"Bonfire anyone?" He held the can above his head.

Bruce frowned. "Son, put that away before I arrest you. You have enough suspicions on your record. Most importantly, why are you out of your house?"

Darla tugged on Bruce's sleeve. "I'm pressing charges, Officer. For defamation of my dead mother's name and for assault."

"You can't defame a drug addict." Stacy laughed; the sound cruel. "They do enough damage to themselves. Why don't you explain to these good people why you don't live with your son?"

19

After Darla knocked Stacy unconscious with a well-placed right hook, leaving the rest of us without the answer to a very intriguing question, Bruce took Darla away in handcuffs, while an ambulance took Stacy. By then, the party was over, and I had a heck of a post for the next gossip column.

Lindsey's friends left in groups. She plopped in a lawn chair and pouted. "Why can't we have a normal evening like other people?"

"Lucky, I guess." I stacked the bowls inside each other, not caring about crushing the chips. They were mostly gone anyway. The buckets of iced soda could wait until morning, but left out food would only attract animals. "But, you're guaranteed to be the most popular kid in school for a few weeks."

She scrunched up her mouth, then nodded, a smile spreading across her face. "You're right. People will fight to come to my next party."

"Hey, what did I miss?" Lynn, my best, but very late friend, strolled up with a glittery pink gift bag in her hand. "Sorry, I couldn't make it earlier. Had a meeting at the school, and tons of papers to grade." She handed the bag to Lindsey. "Happy Sweet Sixteen, sweetheart."

Lindsey got to her feet and gave Lynn a hug. "Thanks. You should have been here. Two of Mom's friends got into a fight and the cops were called."

Technically, Bruce didn't constitute 'cops', and the two women definitely didn't rank as friends, but Lynn would've loved the drama. "I'll tell you all about it once I get this stuff cleaned up."

"Can't wait." She took the bowls from my hand. "Where's that hunky man of yours?"

"Off with my hunky man," Mom said, carrying a couple of folding chairs. "They're out front shooting the bull about tonight's fiasco when they should be out here doing this."

Lynn laughed, shoved the bowls back at me, and then took the chairs from Mom. "We'll get it done faster anyway, then we'll have time to talk."

Maybe so, but I'd been looking forward to some snuggle time with Duane while unwinding from the stress of the evening. Oh, well. Girl time with my bestie was the next best thing. She'd been so busy lately, I hadn't had time to pick her brain on this latest mystery. Other than Duane, she was the smartest person I knew.

By the time we finished cleaning, it was close to eleven p.m and every bone in my body ached. With an ice cold diet soda in my hand and a bowl of

M&Ms to share, I plopped into a chair. By this time, Lindsey had disappeared somewhere with her cell phone, and Duane and Leroy had joined the women.

Since they did end up taking down tables and chairs, I offered each of them a drink. The night had cooled considerably, reminding me that fall was on the horizon. Before I could get up to get a blanket, Duane draped a crocheted afghan across my knees. "Thank you." He was the greatest thing ever.

"Hey, where's mine?" Lynn tossed her hair and batted her eyelashes. "I'll be the Maid-of Honor at your wedding. Treat me nice."

He tossed her one from a stack on an empty chair. "Only Marsha gets special treatment."

"I'll have to do something evil to you during wedding preparations." Lynn grabbed the blanket and spread it across her. "If y'all ever get married, that is."

"Shut up, Lynn." I punched her playfully in the shoulder. "I'm working on it."

"Not fast enough." Duane peered over his glass of tea. The sparkle left his eyes.

My heart plummeted. Was he getting tired of waiting? Would I, if I were in his shoes? The subject needed changing immediately. I averted my gaze. "So, what do y'all think the answer to Stacy's question was?"

"I need to know the question first," Lynn pointed out. "You haven't told me what happened at the party." She almost busted a rib laughing as I filled her in on the night's happenings.

"Shut up and tell me whether you know what Stacy was talking about." I couldn't help but laugh with her. In hindsight, it was a humorous evening.

"I've heard rumors, but that's all they are, and I don't like to gossip." She tipped her soda can to her mouth.

"It's not gossip in a situation like this." I put a hand on her arm. "Someone is trying to kill me."

"It's true," Duane admitted. "We're not happy about it, but someone definitely tried to shoot Marsha the other night, and she's worried Dottie only has a week to live."

"I'm your best friend, and you didn't tell me someone shot at you?" Lynn widened her eyes.

"Sorry, but I had enough people worrying about me." It seemed suspicious that Mom sat silently a few feet away not saying anything. Something had to be going through her brain. Her mind was like a computer with too many browser windows left open. "What's on your mind, Mom?"

"Well, I think I might know what Lynn is going to say, and trying to figure out if I want to spill the information or not. I don't want to be labeled a gossip any more than she does."

I gulped my drink in order not to snort. Mom couldn't keep a secret to save her life. "How did you come by this information?"

"The quilting club. How else? Those women know everything about everybody in this town."

"Why haven't you said anything before?" I'd never known her to sit on anything juicy for longer than a day.

"I know I flap my lips more than I should…" She glared at Leroy when he snorted. "But I do make sure the information has some truth to it first. That's why I haven't said anything. I haven't had time to do my research."

"It's getting late, Mom." Despite drooping eyelids, I sat straighter in my chair, eager to hear her news. "Tell me and we can research together."

"Stacy is correct in saying Darla's mother was a drug addict. So was Darla, to be honest. She lost custody of her son when Danny was a teenager. When he turned eighteen, he disappeared for a while and lived up in Little Rock somewhere. Him and Darla came to River Valley within a few weeks of each other. No idea why Danny chose to live with his father's parents, considering his dad left Darla when he was a little boy." Mom upended her glass, finishing her tea, then set the glass on the grass at her feet.

"You'd think with Darla being so controlling, she would've insisted he stay with her." Mom shrugged. "Anyway, Darla's mother overdosed. Lay undiscovered for a week before a neighbor noticed the smell."

What a tragic story. "What's Stacy's part in all this? There has to be a reason the two women hate each other. Something more than Amber getting pregnant."

A mysterious smile flickered at Mom's mouth. For someone who didn't want to air someone else's dirty laundry, she sure seemed to be enjoying herself.

"You're having fun, aren't you?" I peered into her face. "How long have you been sitting on this juicy bit of news?"

"Since yesterday." Mom shrugged. "The women talk, especially as they're packing up to leave. I guess they don't think I can hear as well then. Anyway, Darla hates Stacy because Stacy stole her husband right after Stacy graduated high school. Most folks think they might've been messing around while she was jail bait, but nothing was proven. Darla's husband broke up with her because she was too old, his words, not mine, and used the same excuse with Stacy. That's why she got the plastic surgery, I reckon. It costs a lot of money to stay young."

Wow. Mom just gave me a lot to decipher. I tilted my can, only to find out it was empty. I didn't need any more caffeine anyway.

Three people made it to the top of my suspect list. Now to find out a way to figure out which of them was a murderer.

After Mom and Leroy went inside and Lynn left to go home, Duane and I moved to my sofa where I snuggled close, putting my head on the spot on his shoulder made just for me. A made-for-television romance played on the TV, but we'd muted the sound, content to just sit in each other's presence.

"What do I do now?" I wanted him to tell me, guide me, point me in the right direction.

"I think you need to go to Bruce with your suspicions."

"What if he laughs at me?"

His chest vibrated. "What are you, twelve?"

"Don't laugh. You know Bruce and I don't see eye-to-eye." Of course, he did tell me he needed all the help he could get because of short staffing, but I knew if he thought I might be in danger even in the slightest by knowing this information, he'd pull me off the case faster than Lindsey slammed a door when grounded. I guess it wouldn't hurt to corner him at church the next day.

"Which of the three do you think is the murderer?" I asked.

"What if none of them are?"

I sat up and peered into his face. "If not one of them, then who? There isn't that many people to choose from."

"I'm going to ask you again," Duane pulled me back down and nestled my head under his chin. "Have you asked God to guide you?"

I knew I'd forgotten something. Prayer was so simple, yet when I had a puzzle to solve, I tended to forget. Instead, I forged ahead like a missile, destroying everything in my path. I sighed. "No, I haven't."

The front door banged open. Lindsey stepped inside, then slammed the door behind her. "I hate Bobby." She stomped past us.

"Wait a minute, young lady." I glanced at the clock, relieved that despite her dramatic entrance, she hadn't broken her twelve o'clock curfew. "Where have you been?"

"I'm not late."

"No, but you didn't tell me where you were going, either."

"Don't you have a GPS on my phone?"

Okay, this conversation was going nowhere fast, and my darling daughter was on the verge of being disrespectful. I straightened. "Let's start over before you get grounded. Have a seat." I motioned toward the empty end of the sofa. "Now, tell me what happened."

She plopped next to me. "A group of us went to Wanda's Diner, just to hang out since the party ended so early. I caught Bobby kissing someone else!" She covered her face. "I really thought we'd get back together."

I exchanged a sympathetic glance with Duane. He kissed the tip of my nose. "I'll leave you two ladies to the romantic stuff and see you in the morning at church."

After he left, I turned back to Lindsey. "Why don't you find another boy, sweet—"

"What!?" She lifted her head and glared at me with red-rimmed eyes. "I don't want another boy. It's not that easy. What if you and Uncle Duane broke up? Would you go right out and find a new man?"

Hopefully, Duane and I were a bit different than a couple of love struck fifteen year olds. Also, had Lindsey forgotten I'd caught her under the bleachers a few days ago? "No, I can't say I would. I'm sorry for that uncaring comment. Who was Bobby kissing?"

"Amber."

20

After a sermon about trusting in the Lord and not leaning on my own understanding, and how submitting to Him would make my paths straight, I stood on the church steps and searched for Bruce. I'd tell him everything I knew, then step back and trust the authorities to handle things the way God wanted.

"Who are you looking for?" Lindsey bumped me with her hip. "Uncle Duane's inside."

"Bruce."

"Why?" Lindsey wrinkled her nose. "I'm surprised he hasn't tried to arrest one of us lately. Every time something goes wrong in this town, he blames it on us."

"He's actually not being too bad this time around." I rose up on my toes. Not only did I want to tell him about my new suspicions, but I wanted to know why he hadn't questioned the newspaper about the early obits. My shoulders slumped.

Who was I kidding? I wasn't going to be able to let this go.

Lindsey growled and flounced away. Well, gosh, I knew she didn't like Bruce much, but I didn't think she needed to be so dramatic…Oh. Bobby strolled by with his arm around Amber's shoulders. He watched Lindsey storm past, then let his arm fall.

I would guess things weren't exactly the way Lindsey thought they were. Once we got home, I'd suggest her and Bobby have a serious conversation. Either they liked each other or they didn't. If they thought things were complicated during high school, wait until they became adults.

"Bruce, wait up." I leaped off the step, grunted as my ankle turned, then limped/hopped my way to his side. Ow, that hurt. Bad. "I have some information for you."

"Can't a man take a day off?"

"When there's a murder to be solved?" Seriously? In a small town like River Valley, the one remaining officer who hadn't left for greener pastures needed to work twenty-four/seven. "Are they going to hire you some help?"

"I got another officer showing up tomorrow." He crossed his arms. "What do you want? I'm starving, and I want to grab a burger from Wanda's before the crowd hits."

"I'll join you." I fished my phone out of my purse and texted Duane where I'd be. "You're driving, right?"

Bruce groaned and headed for a raised black SUV. Why did men of short statures drive such big vehicles?

Grabbing a hold of the door frame, I hoisted my short self onto the passenger seat. My ankle would hate me when I jumped out of the monster truck. The ground looked a mile down.

Bruce turned the key in the ignition. "I don't know why we couldn't just meet at the diner."

I pulled a hand full of papers and assorted food wrappers from under me and started a new pile on the floor behind us. "Why? You're right here. Are you afraid I'm going to highjack your truck?"

"I never know what you're going to do. You should wear a warning sign around your neck." He pulled onto the highway that ran through the middle of town.

"You really should have tried your hand at standup comedy, because you are a riot." I glared out the window. Here I was trying to help him and all he could do was insult me. "Police work is really a waste of your—" I caught a glimpse of Amber ducking behind a building. Seconds later, Darla followed her. "Pull over."

"Nope. Hungry, remember?"

"But something seems fishy." What if Darla intended to do Amber harm and we did nothing? "Seriously, Bruce, we need to stop."

"Give me one good reason."

"I'm going to throw up."

He swerved so fast, my seatbelt locked into place and cut into my neck. God, forgive me for the white lie. As soon as we stopped, I thrust open my door and slid out, letting my uninjured foot take the brunt of my weight. "Come on, Bruce."

"I thought you were sick." He slammed his door.

"No, I lied. Sorry. But, I think someone is in danger."

"Do I need my gun?" He stopped and half-turned back to the truck.

"No time!" I grabbed his arm and dragged him along after me. I careened around the corner I'd seen Amber and Darla take and skidded to a halt.

Bruce crashed into me. "What are we doing?"

"I saw Darla following Amber in a suspicious manner."

Shaking his head, he sighed and turned away. "I'm going to eat." He stormed back to his vehicle, me hobbling along after him.

"You'll understand more when I tell you what I know."

"Save it for lunch. I can't listen to you on an empty stomach."

Sometimes he was so dense. If something happened to Amber, I'd never let him forget about putting his stomach first. Grumbling under my breath, I climbed back into the truck and kept my mouth shut until we got to Wanda's.

Bruce seemed happy with my silence as he climbed from behind the wheel and rushed into the diner without waiting for me. If his mother were still alive, I'd be talking to her about her son's lack of gentlemanly manners.

By this time, my ankle throbbed and was turning beautiful shades of blue and purple. Hunger gnawed at my belly. I gritted my teeth and limped after my reluctant lunch date.

The din of Wanda's on a Sunday afternoon rivaled a closely scored football game held inside a concrete building. Voices practically shouted in order to be heard across tables. Wanda squeezed between crowded tables.

Bruce whirled with a frown on his face. "Look how crowded they are. It'll take an hour to get a table."

"There're two stools at the lunch counter." I gave him a shove. "Go! And don't forget to save me a seat. I still need to talk to you."

Bruce sprinted for the stools, almost running over Wanda. She shrieked and whirled. He ducked one way, then dodged another. She spun in a circle. The platter holding glasses of tea and soda flew into the air and shattered to the floor. "Bruce Barnett!" Wanda picked up the platter and whacked him on the head.

"That's assaulting a police officer!" Bruce rubbed the top of his head.

"You're not in uniform." She looked as if she'd hit him again, but instead, stomped back to the kitchen. Seconds later, Bobby came out with a broom and dustpan.

When had Wanda hired him? I skirted around the mess of drinks and glass and perched on the stool beside Bruce. "You really must be starving."

"I ought to arrest her."

I rolled my eyes. "You shouldn't have raced across the diner like a little kid." Grabbing my menu, I hid behind it and grinned, wishing I would've had time to grab my phone and record the crazy dance between Bruce and Wanda. "Are you ready to listen to me, now?"

"Yes." He told the girl behind the counter he wanted a cheeseburger with everything, fries, and a coke.

I ordered a BLT and filled Bruce in on what Mom had told me the night before. He sat quietly while I talked, rubbing his finger across his little Hitler moustache. The gesture freaked me out. What was he trying to prove? Bruce couldn't look tough if the world would end unless he did. By the time I'd finished telling him everything I could think of, our food had arrived and Bruce dug into his without speaking.

"Well?" I cut my sandwich in half. "Don't you think all three of them have a motive?"

"To kill each other, maybe." He dumped an obscene amount of ketchup on his plate. "But how does this info pertain to our deceased old ladies?"

Hmmm. It didn't, when he put it that way. But I knew it all tied together somehow. It had to. Darn Barney, uh, Bruce, for bursting my bubble. Now, I was back to square one. At least in the aspect of Bruce not listening to my concerns and taking me seriously.

"Do you have any other suspects?" I asked.

"No, and no one else has died." He bit into his hamburger, ketchup squeezing out between the patties and landing on his plate with a plop.

"Dottie has a week, Bruce. One week for us to find her killer." I tossed my sandwich on my plate, appetite gone. The woman was cantankerous, man-hungry, opinionated, and her cologne shriveled every living plant she passed, but the world wouldn't be the same without her.

Forcing myself back to eating, I cut a sideways glance at Bruce. "What are you thinking about? You look like you're in another world."

"Just piecing together what you've told me. Maybe I'll have the new guy run background checks on everyone when he arrives tomorrow."

"So, you do believe me?"

"I didn't say that. Just that I'll have him check into things." He tossed his napkin on his empty plate. "Can you find your way home, or do I have to give you a ride?"

Spotting Duane through the plate glass window, I shook my head. "I've got a ride, thanks." I grinned and waved my sweetie over as he entered the diner and Bruce left.

"My dining companion just improved a hundred times over." I raised my face for a kiss.

Duane chuckled. "I have to admit, your text surprised me. You and Bruce tend to rub each other the wrong way. How'd he take to your information?"

"Not good at first, but then he agreed to look into it." I glanced at the clock hanging on the opposite wall. One o'clock. Mom and Leroy must've decided not to do their usual Sunday lunch.

The bell over the door jingled, and Darla and her boyfriend waltzed in and over to an empty booth not far from us, without waiting for the hostess to seat them. Some people thought they owned the world.

"I am not in the mood." Wanda grabbed a couple of menus and marched over to the newcomers.

I met Duane's amused gaze and shrugged. Today had definitely been entertaining. "I took your advice, prayed about today's sermon, and decided to let Bruce handle everything." I hoped he'd handle it before Dottie met her maker.

"I'm proud of you." Duane caressed my cheek, then tucked a loose strand of hair behind my ear. "Anything else you've been praying—"

"We're out of pie, Darla. We run out very quickly after church." High spots of color appeared on Wanda's cheeks.

"Then you should plan for such a shortage." Darla tossed her menu on the table. "I guess I'll have the rhubarb."

"We're out. All we have is a few slices of lemon meringue or pecan."

I glanced around the diner, noticing for the first time how low on help she was that day. Where was everyone? I hadn't waited tables since high school, but unless we wanted to witness Wanda losing her temper, I thought I'd better volunteer. "I'm going to go help. Love you." I planted a peck on Duane's cheek and grabbed a handful of menus before rushing to greet a family of five coming in the front door.

My greeting lacked grace, considering my ankle still throbbed and was growing more painful. Since I had yet to see how swollen it was, I had no idea whether a visit to Urgent Care was in the future. "Welcome to Wanda's. Follow me, please."

"Why are you limping?" Duane asked as I moved past him for glasses of water.

"I fell off the church steps and twisted my ankle."

He shook his head and stood. After guiding me back to my stool, he grabbed a tray with five glasses and a pitcher of ice water. "Sit. I'll do this. Watch and see what a man can do." He winked and strolled away, leaving my heart doing somersaults.

Wanda got teary eyed when she spotted her new handsome waiter and patted his cheek. "God bless you, Duane Steele. Everyone's out with the flu today, and I'm about to have a heart attack."

"We don't want our prettiest business owner keeling over on us, now do we?" He flashed her a dimpled grin, gave another wink at me, and went to soothe Darla's ruffled feathers.

I could sit and watch him move all day. Except for the fact my ankle was killing me. Once Duane finished, we'd definitely be heading to the emergency room.

Two hours later, I played a game on my cell phone and waited for Duane to help Wanda with the last of the afternoon rush. I'd already taken my daily allotment of ibuprofen and my stomach hurt. Not to mention the fact I needed to use the restroom after three large iced teas.

Just when I'd decided to brave the pain and make my way to the restroom, Bruce's SUV sped by, siren wailing, with a magnetic flashing light sitting on top.

21

With one glance at Duane, who obviously could read my mind by now because he handed the menus to Wanda, I hobbled for the door. "Marsha. Marsha!" I ignored his calls and banged the door open. Yep, Bruce's car headed in the direction I'd seen Amber disappear hours ago.

"Come on." Biting back the pain in my ankle, I hurried to Duane's truck.

Duane caught up with me, tossed me in his truck, then dashed to the driver's side. "Do we know where we're going?"

"I'm pretty sure. Drive toward the hardware store." Of course, I could be wrong. Bruce could simply be on his way to a car accident, but instinct told me otherwise. "We have company." I pointed behind us to where other diner customers, Darla and her friend included, jumped into vehicles.

"That's small town life for you." Duane thrust the truck into drive and sped off. "Not enough excitement, so folks chase cops."

I giggled. My life had plenty of excitement, especially since the sleep walking debacle last year.

"We'll go see what's going on, but then I'm taking you to have a doctor look at your ankle." Duane glanced at my leg. "It's a lovely shade of eggplant."

That wasn't a good thing to hear. I loved that particular color, but not on any of my body parts. "Agreed."

Less than five minutes later, we pulled across the street from an ambulance. Two EMTs wheeled a gurney, burdened by a body bag, from around the corner. Bruce trotted beside them, scribbling on his ever present pad of paper. "Can you go see who's on the gurney, please?" My gut told me the answer, but I prayed I was wrong.

Duane sighed and opened his door. "I guess Bruce will yell less if it's me."

Very true. Duane still had a ways to go before Bruce lost his patience with him. Plus, Duane towered over the officer by a head, and his muscles alone were as big as Bruce's legs. Maybe intimidation played a factor in how he related to my fiancé.

I rolled down my window in case a few words drifted my way and leaned out as far as I deemed safe. The doorframe dug into my stomach, but I still couldn't hear a thing. The pain from my foot was starting to make me nauseous, so going for information myself was out of the question.

Settling back on my seat, I texted Duane. "Well?" Then watched him through the window.

He frowned and shook his head. Maybe I'd jumped the gun, but my nerves were strung tighter than a guitar string, and I really thought I might lose my lunch from pain.

My cell phone sang out a jaunty tune about a text message arriving. It was Duane. "The body is Amber's."

My heart sank. I hung my head out of the window and threw up. Poor Amber. And her with a baby on the way. Once I had control of myself again, I texted Duane to send Bruce over.

"He said he's busy."

"He needs to listen to me," I replied.

"He said he'll get your statement later. Maybe at the hospital. I'm coming now."

Ugh. Waiting was the hardest thing ever. I watched plenty of crime shows on television. I knew the first forty-eight hours were the most important, and the killer was walking past Duane's truck at the moment. I would bet my favorite pair of overalls that Darla Quincy killed Amber so her son's name wouldn't be sullied.

"Ready?" Duane slid back behind the wheel. "You okay?"

"I got sick."

"I saw that." He brushed back my hair. "Pain pretty bad?"

"Horrible," I whispered, using the back of my hand to wipe perspiration from my upper lip.

He frowned and sped toward the hospital twelve miles away. Every bump in the road sent waves of pain up my leg. What a dunce. Instead of interrogating Bruce at the diner, I should've had him take me to the ER. But, the pain had increased over time. At first, it'd been hardly noticeable, but hobbling around hadn't helped.

Being a natural klutz, spraining an ankle or getting bruises and not remembering how I got them was a regular occurrence. Surely, nothing was broken.

The doctor clipped the x-ray to his lighted board on the wall. "Looks like you have a fracture. A small one, but it's there. Want a cast, or can I trust you with a sturdy boot?"

Duane snorted. "Better do the immoveable cast. She isn't known for taking things easy."

Tears stung my eyes. My first broken bone. I laid back on the bed and stared at the ceiling. "I want fluorescent pink." I might as well look good while I clumped around.

"I can put a rubber heel on so you don't have to use crutches," the doctor offered. "The break isn't a bad one, but it definitely didn't help with you walking on it all day."

"That would be great, thanks." Keeping Dottie safe, finding out whether Darla killed Amber, and helping Mom in the store seemed like an insurmountable task now.

Duane left to get something to drink, and I closed my eyes, letting the pain pill make me fuzzy.

"You got something to tell me?" Bruce entered the room as the doctor started wrapping the cast.

"In private, please, Doc?" Once the doctor left, I rolled onto an elbow, the pain meds I'd been given dulling the pain in my ankle. "When we were headed to Wanda's for lunch, I saw Darla and Amber duck around the corner of the Hardware store. It appeared as if Darla were following Amber. Now, Amber is dead. I tried to talk to you about it then, but all you could think about was putting food in your stomach."

He raised his eyebrows. "Are you saying Darla killed Amber?"

"I'm saying you should consider the possibility."

"Darla was at the diner with us."

I rolled my eyes. "What time was Amber killed?"

"Sometime between ten and one o'clock."

"So, Darla could easily have killed her then headed to the diner." Did the man not think for himself? I knew he was busy, but everyone was.

"Well," Bruce shrugged. "We aren't even sure it was murder. There are no defensive wounds on the victim, and no other signs of violence."

"Then, how did she die?"

"It looks like she fell and hit her head, but the ME will know more when he's examined her. Is that all?"

I nodded, wondering how I could get off the bed and down to the basement where the morgue was. If the poor girl hit her head, she had help. She wasn't far enough along in her pregnancy to show, much less be unwieldy. No, the circumstances were too suspicious for me to brush off as easily as Bruce seemed to be able to do.

"I've already told you more than I should have." He snapped his notebook closed, not having jotted down a single note, and laughed. "But at least with your foot in a cast, I won't have to worry about you sticking your nose where it doesn't belong."

I failed to mention to him that I would receive a walking cast. Once I wasn't loopy from meds, I'd be as good as new.

Once he left, the doctor and Duane came back in. The doctor finished my cast and an hour later, Duane drove me home. "I know you're itching to find out more details about what happened today, but please let it rest until tomorrow. Give your ankle one day of peace."

Since the day was almost over, that wouldn't be a problem.

Duane drove me home and carried me into the house. After setting me on the sofa, fluffing pillows behind me and placing an afghan across my legs, he handed me the television remote. "It's your lucky day. We can watch any chick flick you want."

"As long as you sit next to me, I don't care what we watch. We can rest my foot in your lap."

"Won't that jostle you?"

"I want you close—"

The front door banged open. "You broke your foot?" Hurricane Lindsey blew into the room. "We can't leave you alone for a minute, Mom. You're a danger to yourself." Tears glimmered in her eyes, showing me that she cared, despite the fists on her thin hips. "I don't want to put you in a nursing home for at least ten more years."

"Gee, thanks." Because every woman wants to go in a home before the age of fifty.

"Sweetie—" Duane reached for her.

"And you!" Lindsey turned with a snarl. "You're going to be her husband. You should take better care of her. First she's shot at, and now…this. Both while *you* were with her." She covered her face with her hands and sobbed.

Duane pulled my daughter into his arms. Her head nestled in the curve of his shoulder, same as mine did when he held me. I smiled through my tears. Although five years old when her father, Duane's brother died, Lindsey couldn't find a better replacement than in the man I intended to marry. Seeing how he related to her, how he soothed her fears, made me reconsider my hesitancy in trying for a second child. Duane would make a wonderful father.

After Lindsey's cries turned to quiet hiccups, Duane led her to the easy chair by the window. He gently sat her down, then knelt in front of her. "I'm sorry your mother was hurt today. Whenever that happens, it rips out my heart. Don't you know how much I want to keep her safe?"

"I know." Lindsey nodded. "Mom makes it difficult."

Duane hid a laugh in a cough and winked at me. "Horribly difficult."

"I'm afraid someone is really going to hurt her bad someday. Like someone did to Amber."

I straightened, knocking one of my pillows to the floor. "Who told you about Amber?"

"Danny." She wiped her eyes on the sleeve of her long-sleeved tee-shirt. "He's pretty upset."

Understandably so, since he's the father of her baby. "Where did you see Danny?"

"Pacing up and down in front of the crime scene tape by Harvey's Hardware." She sniffed. "Once he found out it was Amber, he was almost inconsolable. Kept saying he's had enough. He acted like a crazy person."

Enough of what was the question of the day. Darn this broken foot of mine, and the medication that kept me woozy. I should be out there hitting the pavement, hunting up clues, and catching a murderer. "Where was Bruce while Danny did his little walk?"

"Staring at everyone who walked by, and yelling at anyone who got too close." She shook her head. "That man is really stressed."

At least her bad attitude was off of me.

"And then Danny's mom showed up and the two went at each other like insane people. Bruce had to pull them apart. They sure don't act like mother and son." She gave Duane a hug. "Thanks. I'm sorry I yelled at you, but Mom scares me to death sometimes."

"Yeah, she scares me, too." He grunted as he got to his feet. "Want me to order pizza?"

"Definitely." She plopped on to the sofa, bumping my leg with her arm. I hissed through my teeth, but kept a smile plastered on my face. If she knew how much pain I was in, she'd start ranting again about my carelessness. "Does Grandma know you've hurt yourself again?"

"Uh." I glanced at Duane.

"I didn't tell her, but then Lindsey managed to find out fast enough." He glanced at his watch.

"The store isn't closed yet. Maybe she's sticking around for a last minute customer."

"Maybe." But it wasn't like her to at least call if she knew. I called Mom's cell phone.

"What?" she whispered. "I'm hot on the trail of a suspect."

"Excuse me?"

"You heard me." Click.

"She hung up on me." I stared at the screen on my phone. "She said she was hot on the trail of a suspect."

"The apple doesn't fall far from the tree, does it?" Duane fished out his own cell phone. "I'll try to see if Leroy knows anything." He punched in numbers, then sighed. "Went to voice mail. Try your mom again."

I did. "Mom, are you chasing a suspect for Amber's death?"

"Amber's dead? God in heaven, help us. No, we're following a suspect in the old lady killings."

22

Time was running out for Dottie.

According to the schedule of prior events, she had two days left to walk this earth. I was rapidly losing any hope of stopping a killer before he or she claimed another victim.

After Mom's fiasco of following two electricians while they drove around in an unmarked panel van the other day, and having Bruce question her when the guys placed a call to the station about a suspicious character tailing them, no one seemed to be doing anything to find the real killer. Now, the day had come to put Amber and her unborn child to rest.

I smoothed my navy pinstriped skirt, and then secured my hair in a barrette away from face. I hated funerals, especially ones for young people.

"Here's your shoe." Lindsey handed me a silver ballet flat.

Since I still wore the cast, Lindsey had appointed herself my guardian, letting me, and anyone within hearing, know that I was incapable of taking care of myself. As much as I loved spending time with my one and only child, her constant hovering drove me bonkers.

"Do you need to lean on me to the car? Is Uncle Duane picking us up? I'm not sure it's a good idea for you to drive."

"I broke my left foot, not the one I drive with." *I will not bite her head off. I will not bite her head off.* "And yes, Uncle Duane should be here any minute." I slipped silver earrings into my ears, then surveyed myself in the mirror.

Not turning to my M&Ms every time I felt stressed had helped a few pounds drop off. Add to that, the fact I'd updated my wardrobe, and I didn't feel as if I'd shame Duane in public. At least not with the way I looked.

"Y'all ready?" Duane called from the front room.

"Yes." Lindsey took my arm and tried leading me like an old woman out of the bedroom.

I rolled my eyes and let her. Someday, she might have to care for me for real. Nothing good could come for dissuading her now.

Duane greeted me with a kiss and took over from my daughter, letting me walk beside him. My man knew what I wanted, and that was mostly independence with a huge dose of love and respect thrown in.

The three of us met up with Mom and Leroy on the church steps. From the amount of cars in the parking lot, half of River Valley had shown up. Funerals always drew a crowd, and folks always said the killer attended the funeral of his victim.

Maybe something would jump out at me that would help put this mystery to rest.

The five of us squeezed into a pew two rows behind Stacy, me sitting on the end so my leg could stick into the aisle. A polished mahogany casket sat on a pedestal, a red swatch of silk draping across one end. Flowers cascaded off the top of the silk. Stacy had spared no expense for her younger sister.

Stacy's cries rose above the soft music being piped in from a hidden speaker. My heart went out to her, no matter how strong our personal differences. I reached over and grabbed Lindsey's hand. We knew the pain of loss.

Dottie slid in behind us and leaned on the pew back. "Well, looks like I'm a goner. Only God can find the culprit in the amount of time I have left."

"There's still hope." Mom patted her hand. "Marsha and I won't sleep until we find the person responsible for all the deaths, Amber included."

"We know who killed Amber!" Stacy whipped around like a cobra. "That…that…Darla should be in jail."

"Not without proof." Mom crossed her arms and got that 'look'. If Stacy were smart, or not blinded by grief, she'd back off.

Dottie stood. "I'm sorry your sister is dead, but I'm still alive, and we need to focus on keeping me that way. Darla isn't smart enough to rig a house to blow up."

"But she can bash somebody in the head." Stacy stood and moved to the aisle.

Duane got up and placed himself between them. "Ladies, please—"

Darla pushed through the church doors and made a beeline for the screaming couple. "How dare you spray paint my car! I can't even drive it with those words on it."

Stacy's lip curled. "How dare you kill my sister."

"You ruined my life years ago, you stupid sl—"

"Hey." Duane put his hands on Darla's shoulders and pulled her back while mouthing for me to call the police. "We don't need to resort to name calling. A little help here, Leroy."

"Nah." He laughed. "I'm kind of hoping to see some hair pulling."

I transferred my attention from one to the other like a spectator at a ping pong tournament. Sure seemed like the hatred between the two ran deep, and they'd veered from the reason we were all gathered. Now that Dottie was out of the skirmish, she stood to the side, arms crossed, head cocked to the side. I'd pay a dollar to know what was going through her wily head. Other spectators watched with wide eyes and open mouths.

Mom smacked Leroy on the shoulder, then scooted past Lindsey, her rounded rump obstructing my view for a moment, before she joined the party in the aisle. "Y'all are making a scene. A young mother-to-be is dead, and all you care about are past grievances."

Flashbulbs went off. Who took pictures at a funeral? I craned my neck, surprised to see Frank Powell. I supposed with money at the newspaper tight, he'd undertaken the role of photographer in addition to his other duties.

"Mind your own business." Darla snarled and yanked free of Duane's grip. She two-hand shoved Stacy hard enough to knock the younger woman to her rear, then turned on Mom. The moment the woman's hand connected with Mom's face, I was out of my seat and into the aisle by the time Stacy resumed her footing.

"Duane, find Bruce." I shoved my way between the fighting women. "No one hits my momma."

"I'm needed here." Duane pinned Darla's arms behind her back and started dragging her toward the door. She cussed and kicked, her hair flying around her face.

"I'll find him." Leroy slid from the pew and dashed out a side door.

I followed my man and his deranged captive to the patch of grass outside the church. When Darla landed a well-aimed kick to Duane's shin, I pinched her upper arm as hard as I could. "Stop it right now!"

Using my sternest 'mom' voice and look, I shook a finger in her face. "This is a funeral. Regardless of your feelings toward the poor young woman who is dead inside, show some respect for the House of God."

Darla froze. Her face crumbled, and she sagged out of Duane's grip. Collapsing to the ground, she covered her face with her hands. "I'm sorry. What came over me? You're right. I'm out of line. There's so much bad blood between Stacy and I.

More than work related competition. More than our love for family members' deaths. Enough drama to fill a book."

I kneeled in front of her. "I know about your husband's infidelity, but today is not the day to air that grievance."

Bruce approached, dangling handcuffs, their clanking filling the air. "Okay, step back."

"No" Darla shook her head, her hands falling to her lap, revealing a face which lacked red eyes or tear tracks. "You can't take me to jail."

"Just long enough for you to cool down," he said. "Stand up and turn around. You'll be out by morning."

By this time, those inside the church had stepped outside, forming a loose circle around us. Mom's cheek still sported the imprint of Darla's hand. I felt no pity for the woman, only thoughts of how a few hours or one night behind bars was not enough for a woman who would cause such a scene at a funeral. Besides, I found it curious that her loud sobbing left no visible traces of grief on her face.

Spotting Danny on the outskirts of the crowd, I headed his way as Bruce led the young man's mother to a squad car. The boy looked like the grief his mother pretended to feel. Eyes bloodshot, face haggard, shoulders slumped under a heavy burden.

I held out my hand. "Have you been inside to say goodbye?"

He shook his head, not taking my hand. I let it drop. "Come with me. I'll make sure no one bothers you."

After taking one glance toward the church, Danny whirled and raced into the trees. Maybe Stacy frightened him more than I thought. Maybe he suffered guilt over Amber's pregnancy. I shrugged. No way of knowing for sure, unless he told me, and I felt pretty sure that wouldn't happen. I clomped my way back to the church, where Duane waited for me by the steps.

"Everything all right?" He put an arm around my shoulders.

I nodded. "He's a very distraught young man."

He nodded and led me back to our seat. Once everyone settled back into their chosen spots, the minister stepped up to the podium. I felt pretty sure he'd never seen a service quite like the one that day.

While he talked about God picking another rose for His garden, my mind wandered. I honestly tried to concentrate, but the events of the last hour swirled through my mind. Something important happened that day…something about the murders… a clue, but I couldn't see what.

I remained in my seat as attendees began to file past the casket. Viewing a dead body left me cold. I'd rather remember Amber as the pretty, but sullen store clerk with heavily made up eyes. Not a wax figure in a box.

Catching a glimpse of Danny skulking outside the open window of the church, I excused myself and clunked my way outside. "Danny." I peered around the corner to see him disappear around another. He'd always seemed a bit sneaky to me, now his actions proved my suspicions correct.

When I got around to the back of the church, Danny stood plastered against the wall, his head turned toward a window. "Who are you waiting for?"

He yelped and whirled, quickly shoving something into his pocket. "Uh, no one. I'm just attending the funeral of my girlfriend and baby."

"Then why not go inside?" I tilted my head.

"That Stacy chick won't want me there."

"True, but she can't legally keep you out."

He frowned and his face darkened. "Maybe not, but she managed to get my mother sent to jail."

"That was your mother's fault." Relax. Don't anger him. Maybe I could get some answers, since he seemed receptive to conversation. "Why don't you live with your mother?"

"My grandparents are alone. It isn't good for old people to live alone."

True, at least recently. "Okay, but that leaves your mother alone."

"She isn't old." He shook his head. "Is there a point to these questions, Mrs. Steele? Because, I'm not in the mood for idle conversation."

"I guess you're not." I stepped closer, then stopped as he stiffened. "I'm sorry about Amber, Danny. They'll find out who killed her."

"What? She wasn't murdered. She fell and hit her head."

"That is what I've heard." I glanced to where people started emerging from inside the church.

"You think someone killed her?" His fists clenched. A steely look came over his face, and I took another step back. "Why do you think that?"

No way was I going to tell this angry young man that I suspected his mother. "I don't know. No one told me the official cause of death. Because of the other deaths, I assumed—"

"Those people were old! Amber is young and beautiful. People will miss her." A drop of spittle hung from his bottom lip. He leaned closer. "She. Fell. And. Hit. Her. Head."

"Understood." I watched him march toward the highway, anger in every line of his trembling body.

23

"I'm coming, Dottie. Your thirty days aren't actually up until tomorrow, and nobody dies before their time." I tossed my slippers into my suitcase and zipped it closed. A shudder ran through me at the thought of two days with the crotchety woman, but a promise was a promise. On the plus side, she was bound to fill my ear with gossip for the column, which I was quitting as soon as the killer was found. Something about airing folks' dirty secrets bothered me.

"Don't act like it's going to kill you."

The fact remained that staying with Dottie could very well kill me. Sure, the victims were all elderly women who lived alone, but what if the killer didn't know I was there and went ahead with his or her diabolical plan to blow us up? It might be difficult with Dottie living in a retirement community, but not impossible.

"How am I going to watch out for you at Dottie's?" Lindsey plopped across my bed.

"You could come with me." I grinned.

"Not in this lifetime. Maybe you could take Grandma with you. Safety in numbers and Grandma is more her age."

I laughed. "Don't let her hear you say that. There's at least a twenty-year age difference between the two."

She shrugged. "Hard to tell. Anyway, what can you possibly do with someone that age?"

"I think we're playing Bingo tonight, after hitting the Senior Early Bird Special at Wanda's." Which I didn't mind, since it'd been a few years since I'd enjoyed a rousing game of Bingo, and any meal at Wanda's was a good one.

"Y'all are really living it up." Lindsey giggled and plucked at a loose thread on my quilt. "I'll make sure to deliver a case of Ensure before your bedtime at six."

"Maybe I should make you come with me."

"No, I'm going to the movies with some friends." She held up a hand as I started to speak. "I'll be home by curfew. I wouldn't want Grandma and Leroy to stay up too late on my account."

And there was my sweet, thoughtful daughter again. Had I been as quick to swing from one mood to the other when I was her age?

"I've been kind of snooping." She pulled harder on a thread.

"Stop that before the whole thing falls apart." I tapped her hand. "What kind of snooping?" My heart lodged in my throat.

"I know how important it is for you to find this person before someone else dies, so I've kind of been asking questions." She gave me a sideways glance.

"Of who?"

"Uh, Danny mostly." She shook her head. "He sure doesn't talk much. I also spent a lot of time browsing the store where Amber worked, although the clothes were a little too old for me." She rolled to her side and rested her head on her hand. "Danny doesn't really like his mother."

No secret there. "How does this pertain to the mystery?"

"I'm not sure, but…" Biting her lip, she exhaled sharply through her nose. "I need to talk to Bruce. I might have seen Amber's killer."

My knees buckled, and I fell to the bed beside her. "Please don't tell me you witnessed her death."

"Not exactly. Oh, Mom!" She threw herself into my arms. "It was awful. I was taking a short cut to Rachel's house by cutting around the back of the shops. I heard a scream, a loud noise, then by the time I got there, Amber was lying in a pool of blood next to the dumpster. It was me that called the ambulance." She cried harder. "I didn't call right away. I was so scared the killer might've seen me. Mom, there's no way she tripped and fell without some help. There wasn't even a puddle to slip in."

I'd come to that same conclusion without seeing her body. I tightened my grip on my daughter. What if the killer had seen her snooping around? We needed to call Bruce immediately. "You're definitely coming with me to Dottie's."

"No, Mom!" She straightened fast enough to cause the top of her head to connect with my chin.

My teeth clanked together with a snap. After making sure I hadn't lost part of my tongue, I took a deep breath. "The killer might have seen you. I want you with me for safety."

She rolled her eyes. "You can't save much with a broken foot. What if we have to run for our lives?"

"Don't be dramatic." I chewed the inside of my cheek, rethinking her staying with me and Dottie. What if that put her in more danger than leaving her here? "Fine, but you're staying by Leroy every second!" Grabbing her hand, I pulled her after me as I marched across the yard to Mom's house.

They sat at the kitchen table, Mom reading a book, Leroy the paper, both with coffee cups in their hands. Mom glanced up with a smile. "Good morning to my beautiful girls."

"Sit." I pointed Lindsey to one of the vacant chairs, then sat in the last one. "It seems, Lindsey might have seen a little more of Amber's murder than she should have."

Mom sighed and got to her feet. "Let me fix you a cup of coffee before you start talking. I'm sure I won't want to miss a single word."

I could've sworn I heard her mutter, "How do they get mixed up in these things?" Since I wasn't sure, I kept my mouth shut.

"All right," Mom said, handing me a coffee heavily laced with chocolate. She then handed Lindsey a hot cocoa. "Spill the beans."

Lindsey shot off at the mouth faster than a dog after a rabbit. By the time she'd finished, Mom and Leroy stared like a couple of barn owls.

"Did you see anyone other than Amber in the alley?" Leroy asked.

"Maybe." Lindsey suddenly concentrated on her drink. "I kind of screamed when I found Amber, then I heard footsteps run off."

"So, the killer could have seen you?" My blood chilled. "If they saw you, then that person could also believe you saw them." I bolted to my feet and grabbed the wall phone. I couldn't dial Bruce's number fast enough.

"What now?" He growled.

"I need you. My mom's house. Now." I hung up and stared at Lindsey's face while I dialed Duane. I repeated my cryptic message, gaining strength from his promise to arrive within ten minutes.

More times than I could count, I'd warned Lindsey of the dangers of cutting behind the stores. That it only took once for disaster to strike. We'd found that one time. My legs trembled and I reached over Mom's refrigerator before remembering I no longer kept my M&Ms there.

"Freezer." Mom motioned her head. "I knew you'd come looking at my house sooner or later. For all of our sanity, I stashed a bag."

"Thank you." *God, please don't let anything happen to my daughter.* I sagged against the counter, clutching my chocolate. Again, I stopped to pray only when against a wall. When all else seemed hopeless and fear filled me.

For the first time, I experienced the same worry my family felt when I rushed into a mystery. I found I didn't like the feeling. Who died and made me savior of the world? The world only needed one, and He was much better equipped than I was. Once this killer was caught, I'd never try to solve another mystery. I tossed several candies into my mouth.

"What happened?" Duane burst through the kitchen door, his handsome face creased and hair mussed. After Leroy filled him in, he headed straight for the coffee pot. "Where's Bruce?"

"Here." In his uniform, Bruce appeared only slightly more authoritative, not instilling a lot of confidence in his ability to keep my baby safe. Again, Leroy repeated the story.

Lindsey continued to stare into her hot chocolate. Mom refilled her coffee. Bruce glanced from me to each of the others. "You Calloway women will be the death of me." He wiggled his fingers at Mom. "Coffee."

She shrugged and handed him her mug, then fetched a fresh cup for herself.

Bruce took the chair I'd vacated and pulled out his notepad. "Could you hear the victim talking with anyone before she screamed?" He narrowed his eyes at Lindsey.

She shook her head. "Just the scream, a loud noise, then running feet. Are they going to come after me?"

"I'll have the new officer patrol in front of your house a couple of times a day, when he isn't running past the retirement home, keeping an eye on Dottie." He flipped the pad closed. "River Valley definitely needs more police officers with this family living here."

"It hasn't always been like this." Not until the women's ministry leader decided she needed money to adopt a little girl from China and didn't care how she came to possess the funds. That was definitely not my fault. The Calloways didn't get involved until she stole from us, Lindsey got blamed, and I found a dead body. Same as in this case. I stumbled upon it. I didn't go looking for danger.

"Do you have any suspects at all?" Duane moved closer to me and slipped his arms around my waist, drawing me close.

"Everyone is a suspect." Bruce's shoulders sagged. "Except for maybe the people in this room."

"I've been wondering...why haven't you questioned Frank about the postings in the obituaries?" I rolled the top of the candy bag and stuck it back in the freezer. "I mean, someone is taking the information off the internet. Maybe they need to start checking their sources."

"No, I haven't spoken to him. I'll do that first thing Monday morning." He stood and patted Lindsey on the head with all the grace of a man unfamiliar with the ways of dealing with children. Or teenagers, for that matter.

Lindsey glared and pulled away. "Just try not to let me get killed, okay?"

"Just stay together. That's my advice for now."

"I can't," I said. "I promised Dottie I'd stay with her through tomorrow. She thinks if someone else is there, then she'll be safe."

"Yeah, guess staying in a jail cell didn't work out so well a month ago." Bruce glanced around the room. "Can't she stay here?"

"Absolutely not," Mom said. "That woman is like a burr in someone's sock."

"I need to switch professions. Maybe one where I don't deal with people." Bruce headed out the door.

A horn blared from out front. One glance out the window showed Dottie waving from her cotton-candy pink Cadillac.

"I'll grab your suitcase." Leroy set his cup in the sink on the way out.

"I don't like you staying with her," Duane said, turning me to face him.

"Do you really think someone will blow up her apartment? That might injure her neighbors. They don't seem to kill willy-nilly."

"No, but if the killer is determined to make Dottie their next victim, he or she could use a different method, and you'd be collateral damage."

"True, but they haven't so far. I'll be alight." I stood on tip toe and gave him a kiss, sounding much braver than I felt.

"I'll be calling you every hour, and you'd better answer your phone."

"Don't call during Bingo. You know how the old ladies get when they can't hear the caller." I grinned and caressed his cheek. "I asked Dottie if you could stay with us, but she said it wouldn't be proper for two single women to spend the night with a man."

He laughed as she honked again. "Well, you'd better rush out to Polly Prude."

"Surprising, since she's known as the tramp of the retirement home," Mom added. "But, I guess even Dottie has standards."

"Stop it." I kissed Duane again, landed a peck on my daughter's cheek, and sauntered out the door, trying to look as if my heart wasn't clogging my throat. *God, please let me see my family again.*

I really didn't want Dottie's wrinkled, heavily made-up face to be the last one I saw on earth.

24

"It's about time, girlie. I thought my time would run out, sitting here waiting for you." Dottie sped backward, thrust the giant car into drive, then roared down the highway. "We should take a road trip. Like Thelma and Louise. Remember that movie?"

I stared at her with nothing less than astonishment. "Didn't they kill some guy and then drive off into the Grand Canyon?"

"Well, we don't have to go to those extremes, but two wild women like us could have quite the adventure."

"I'm having a big enough adventure right now, thank you." One I didn't care to repeat or have drag on much longer. Most people who had the threat of less than twenty-four hours to live wouldn't be quite as joyful as my companion. I'd be holed up somewhere, praying harder than ever before.

"Once we get you settled in my apartment, we'll head over to Wanda's. Early Bird starts at four and Bingo at six. We don't want to be late for either one."

All I had was an overnight bag, so settling in would take all of five minutes. Oh, and I'd borrowed my mom's Bingo bag of assorted colored daubers. My favorite was the fluorescent pink heart. Hopefully, it would bring me good luck.

With much maneuvering and backing up to start over, Dottie finally managed to park her pink behemoth into her designated parking space. Since she didn't have medical needs or need a nurse on a regular basis, she rented one of the independent living apartments.

"I love this place," she said, opening her door. "There's always something going on. Not to mention there's a couple of foxy men living here." She winked before closing her door.

I shook my head, reached over the seat to grab my bag, then joined her on the sidewalk. "I'm glad you're active."

"How else do you think I keep my girlish figure?" She sashayed toward the staircase. "One of my secrets is to never take the elevator if I don't have to. Another is weekly ballroom dance lessons. Too bad I don't have one tonight. Visitors get a free lesson. You could practice for your wedding."

"Yeah, too bad." I followed her up three flights of stairs, breathing like an overweight basset hound, while Dottie acted as if she did nothing more than stroll down the sidewalk. A fancy well-choreographed dance at the wedding might be fun, and the lessons might help get me in better shape.

After an eternity of stairs, Dottie stopped in front of her apartment and opened the door, ushering me into a dream room...for a little girl of six. Everything was pink! Pink carpet, pink slipcovers, pink, pink, pink. It looked like a bottle of Pepto-Bismol exploded. Already, I felt hives coming on. "Wow, this is…very feminine."

"Men like a girly woman, Marsha. Remember that. If you always look and act like a girl, Duane will never stray."

I'd prefer to act like a woman, but I got the message, and thankfully, I was pretty sure Duane would never allow me to go all pink. I dropped my bag near the sofa. "Okay, let's go. Wanda's is waiting."

"It's too early. Have a seat, and I'll fix you a glass of lemonade." She bustled away around a wall to where I presume a small kitchen sat.

I perched on the edge of the sofa and tried to let my gaze fall on something that didn't make me want to throw up. A small framed print over a flat screen television drew my attention. Although the sand in the beach scene had a pinkish tint, at least the waves and palm trees broke up the monochromatic color scheme.

"Here you go." Dottie handed me a glass of pink lemonade. "You should take a look around the place. Each room is a different color scheme."

I sipped the too sweet drink. "How many rooms are there?"

"Three, not counting the kitchen. I carried the pink theme through there, with accents of white and dashes of mint green. Very lovely. Take a look later. The bathroom is canary yellow and my bedroom is lime green." She beamed. "I've thought of doing interior decorating as a part-time job, but my other activities keep me way too busy."

So that explains her all pumpkin-colored outfit. No one had ever told Dottie that clothes, and furnishings, needed to go together, not match exactly. "Very clever."

"I've been told that many times." She glanced at the clock. "Time to go." After snatching my unfinished drink from my hand, she rushed back to the kitchen, then dashed for the front door. "There'll be a line forming at the diner, and we mustn't be too far back."

Gracious. I was exhausted already, and I hadn't been with her for a full hour yet.

"Don't forget your Bingo markers!" She stampeded down the stairs, leaving me to close the door.

Fifteen minutes later, we stood outside Wanda's Diner, a half-hour early for the Early Bird. If anyone over the age of fifty-five walked up, Dottie made sure to tell them we were in line for the Special. My face flamed, and I gave so many sheepish grins, my cheeks hurt and my jaw popped.

"You didn't lock my front door, did you?" Dottie peered at me.

"No. It wasn't locked when we arrived, so I figured you preferred it that way."

"Usually I lock it, but with Nina's and Mae's houses exploding when they *unlocked* their doors, I'm not taking any chances."

This time, I couldn't fault her reasoning. At four o'clock exactly, Dottie pushed open Wanda's front doors and waltzed up to the hostess station. "The Early Bird Special, please."

The young lady behind the oak podium styled structure frowned at me. "She isn't old enough for the special, but I'll seat you anyway."

Well, pooh. I would've enjoyed a little discount after the crazy 'Alice in Wonderland' type of day I was having. "That's okay. I'll pay full price."

Dottie patted my arm. "That's sweet of you to offer to pay. How generous."

I sighed and followed the hostess.

We repeated the whole hurry up and wait process when we moved to the bingo hall across town. Were all of the elderly this paranoid? I thought for a minute of the older folks I knew. Nope. Just Dottie.

A long line stretched from the Knights of Columbus building. Already my feet and back ached from standing at Wanda's and my thighs cried out for mercy from climbing the stairs. Maybe I should join a gym. Then, I could buy one of those skinny wedding dresses.

"Clara!" Dottie grabbed my elbow and dragged me to the front of the line. "There you are."

"Who's Clara?" I yanked free.

"Just play along." Dottie grinned and squeezed in behind a stout man. She jumped up and down on her tip toes, hooting and hollering to rival any carnival caller. "Oh, pooh, she can't hear me. Wait over there, Marsha, and I'll be right back." Still talking several decibels too loud, she shoved me out of the line, causing me to stumble because of my cast. Surely no one believed her ruse. They must all be used to her.

I was beginning to see why my mother avoided her if at all possible. I pulled my text phone out of my pocket and texted Duane. "This woman is nuts."

"Where are you?"

"Bingo."

"Win."

I smiled, and texted back, "I'll try. Love you."

"Ditto."

Feeling warm and fuzzy, I slipped the phone back in my pocket and noticed Dottie waving and glaring at me from the cashier's table. "Sorry," I said, rushing to her side. "Got a phone call."

"We almost lost our spot in line." She explained the complicated procedures of serious Bingo. Nobody bought only one set of sheets. Instead, they bought three, plus any of the specialty games. Everyone had several types of snacks and a soda or sweet tea in front of them. By the time we finished, I'd spent thirty dollars. Not exactly cheap entertainment.

Dottie led me to a table close to a raised platform and slid into a chair before a poor woman with a cane could take the seat. I shook my head and mouthed my apologies. The other woman patted my hand and shrugged. Obviously, they were all use to Dottie's shenanigans.

"Everyone knows this is my seat." She raised her nose in the air. "Yet, every week someone tries to take it."

"It doesn't have your name on it." I pulled out the chair next to her.

"It's the same as church, Marsha. If you sit in a pew more than once, it becomes yours. That's in the Bible." She set out ten different daubers and a stuffed chicken. "For good luck."

Not wanting to argue with her about what was or was not in the Bible, I set out my daubers in imitation and reached into my purse for a little plastic frog I carried with me. "Fully Rely On God," I told her with a grin. "Get it? Frog. F.R.O.G."

"I got it. I'm not ignorant."

And the first number was called. B-12.

As the night wore on, and each game neared the end, the rumbling of the crowd grew louder. I couldn't help but be drawn into the excitement. By the time the last game, a blackout, started, I'd won nothing, had a pounding headache, and my stomach ached from all the snacks. I marked the called spots half-heartedly, until the caller said O-69. "Bingo!" I leaped to my feet, shaking my paper. "Bingo. I got a Bingo." Oh, my, goodness, I'd just won twelve hundred dollars.

"Beginner's luck." Dottie racked her belongings into her bag. "Biggest pot ever and a newcomer wins. It ain't fair."

"It's because of my frog." I grinned and waited while a woman verified my numbers, and then a man in a yellow striped vest brought me my check.

"Hurry up." Dottie pushed past me. "Let's go. I'm tired and ready for bed."

My smile didn't fade through the congratulations of the other players, nor did it falter as I followed a poor loser to her big pink car. I had money for a humdinger of a wedding dress.

Tomorrow, I'd look at the calendar and see if I could come up with a date. Maybe spring time. Then, we could have an outdoor wedding out by the lake.

"Stop grinning like a fool and get in the car." Dottie slammed her door.

"What happened to Thelma and Louise?"

"Shut up." She put the car in reverse, then drive and squealed tires out of the parking lot. "I'm dropping you off at the apartment while I run to the corner store for some cereal. That okay with you for breakfast?"

I glanced at my watch. She'd never be home by midnight. "Can't I go with you?"

"Nope. Gotta get some personal stuff, too."

"Okay." I'd just wait in the parking lot until she returned. No way would I head upstairs and wait for an explosion. "Don't be gone long. We're supposed to stay together."

"Don't suffocate me. I've lost older friends for less reasons."

My, she didn't take losing well. I shrugged and stared out the window. We stopped at the entrance to the retirement home and waited while Danny shuffled his way past. The young man's shoulders were in their usual slump. He never looked toward us, seemingly lost in his own world. Poor thing. A mother like Darla, and now the loss of his girlfriend and child. My heart ached for him.

"Get out right here. No sense in me pulling in then back out."

I did as instructed and hobbled my aching self toward the second stairwell. Thirty minutes later, I still sat there, my elbows folded on my knees, my head resting on my arms. Where did Dottie get her energy? After midnight and the woman still roamed the town.

Sirens wailed, and an ambulance and the town's one squad car sped past

25

Having called Duane to pick me up and drive out to where the ambulance and police car sat, we then followed the ambulance to the hospital. Dottie hadn't returned to her apartment because she'd wrapped her pink Caddy around a tree.

Duane and I now sat in the waiting room of St. Mary's Hospital, the smell of antiseptic and sickness permeated the rooms. Soft beeping and the sound of padded shoes filled the air. Somewhere out of sight, a woman wept.

"An eye witness said Dottie swerved and crashed at approximately twelve fifteen," Duane said. "She was headed back to the apartment."

"The killer got to her despite me staying with her." Acid churned in my stomach.

"We don't know that."

"Yes, I do. My gut tells me I'm right." I stared at the tile under my feet. A chipped corner broke up the black and white pattern. The hospital could use a dose of Dottie's flamboyant colors.

Duane grabbed my hand. "She isn't dead, Mars-Bars." He gave me a sad smile, knowing how much I disliked that nickname, but also knowing I'd welcome it at a time like this one. "The killer, if that's the case, may not have succeeded here. Bruce said he'd be here as soon as he could to fill us in on what they found at the scene."

I nodded, praying Dottie would survive the attack against her. Murderers veered from their MOs all the time. It definitely wasn't unheard of.

Hard footsteps echoed across the floor. Bruce stopped in front of us, tapping his notebook against his palm. "Y'all step outside with me. I won't discuss the investigation in here."

Duane helped me to my feet. We followed Bruce to the Emergency room exit. He continued tapping the notebook, as if he were trying to decide how much to tell us. "Okay. Best we can figure is that Dottie's brake line was cut when she stopped at the liquor store."

"Liquor store?" That little old woman was full of surprises.

"At first, we thought maybe it was a case of drunk driving, but the garage mechanic said the line was definitely cut." He narrowed his eyes at me. "If you breathe one word of this to anyone, I will throw you in jail. We can't let the suspects think we know more than them."

"Ah-ha! So you do have a suspect."

Bruce sighed. "Getting close, but I'm not going to divulge that information. As much as it pains me to admit, you're smart. Think long and hard. You'll figure it out." He spun on his heel and marched to where he'd parked his squad car.

"What do you think he has?" I stepped against Duane, using his body heat to ward off the autumn chill. "An anonymous phone call? A fingerprint?"

He steered me back inside. "Let's just worry about Dottie right now, okay?"

"You're right." I took a seat in the same chair as before and stared through the large window at the dark parking lot. What if I'd been in the car with her? Would the killer still have cut the brake line since my name wasn't mentioned in the obit, or would I have been collateral damage? Good thing I was sitting down because my legs would've failed me. Lindsey had no idea how close she had come to being an orphan.

Due to the late hour, my eyelids drooped. I rested my head on Duane's shoulder and he rested his head against mine. I woke to the doctor shaking me.

"Mrs. Steele?" He grinned as I popped up, banging my head on Duane's cheekbone. "None of that, now. We don't need to be stitching either of you up."

I leaped to my feet. "How's Dottie?"

"She'll be fine. A concussion, some minor lacerations. She's a tough old bird. She also listed you as responsible party since she has no living relatives. She'll be released by noon tomorrow and will need a ride." He handed me a clipboard with a page needing my signature.

Sweet old thing, thinking of me as family. I scrawled my name, more than ready to go home and fall into my bed. I'd also need to head to work in a few hours. I'd left Mom to mind the store alone for long enough. Wait. No, today was Sunday and the store was closed. Wonderful. I could sleep until Monday.

Less than a half-hour later, I lay in my bed covered with a thick quilt. I stared wide-eyed through the dark room toward the ceiling. Was it possible to be too tired to sleep? My mind ran like a marathon sprinter, while my body tried to become one with the mattress.

"Marsha!" I woke by being shook up like a milkshake. My eyes popped open and I blinked like a new puppy at Mom's face.

"What?" I tossed off the blanket and sat up fast enough to make my head spin.

"Look." She threw the newspaper at me. "The killer isn't following standard operating procedure."

"You watch too many cop shows." I scanned the sheet. My heart stopped. "Why would your name be here?" She didn't live alone. She was married with a family. "Someone thinks we know who they are. They're playing with us. Letting us know the game is coming to an end."

Mom planted her fists on her hips. "Right after we talk to Bruce, I want you to march over to that newspaper and ask Frank, who we just saw at the funeral, why he would allow this to be printed."

Fear ran through my veins like ice water. "We need to have a family meeting." Since I still wore the clothes from yesterday, all I needed to do was slip my uncasted foot into one of my fuzzy bunny house shoes. I shuffled down the hall to wake up

Lindsey. From that moment forward, no one was to be alone. Not even to use the bathroom. Someone could wait outside the door.

"Family meeting. Mom's name is in the obits. Hurry up." I tossed aside Lindsey's blankets. She was out of bed in a split second.

"Let's go find us a killer." She grabbed a pair of sweat pants and pulled them on over the boy boxers she slept in. "It's personal now."

Great. As if Mom wasn't enough to worry about.

I hurried after my daughter as fast as my broken foot would allow. By the time we barged into the kitchen, Mom had coffee perking and Duane and Leroy were sitting, stony faced, at the table. Not two men I'd want to mess with.

"Has anyone called Bruce?" I sat across from my honey.

"No. He's done nothing helpful yet." Duane's brow dipped lower.

Whoa. Bruce just lost his strongest ally. "I still think he should know about this."

"I'll call him." Mom set five mugs on the table and started pouring. "I want to see his face when he realizes that his late mother's best friend is about to die." Her hand shook, spilling some coffee onto the table.

Leroy placed his hand over hers. "I won't let that happen, darling."

"You might not be able to prevent it."

"Oh, I'll prevent it, all right. No one goes after my woman without a fight."

"We're losing focus here." Duane leaned forward and folded his hands on the table. "This is a direct invitation to find this person. They've stepped out of the norm to target Gertie."

"What do you suggest we do?" My stomach rebelled at the thought of coffee or anything else put inside it. Instead, I swirled the dark liquid and let my mind try to process through the information I knew, in hopes of pinpointing a murderer. Very difficult to do, when everyone expressed their outrage and opinion all at the same time.

The noise level reached dangerous levels when a piercing blow on a whistle put an end to it all. Bruce marched into the kitchen. "I heard y'all from the driveway."

Mom slapped him in the chest with the rolled up paper. "You can arrest me for assault after you read that."

"Why would I arrest you?" Bruce smoothed out the paper.

"Because, I'm going to punch you in the mouth for not finding this person by now." Mom stomped her foot. "Your poor mother must be rolling over in her grave."

"Leave my mother out of this." He scanned the page, his eyes widening. "Heaven have mercy." He took a shaky breath and fixed his gaze on Mom. "You'll be fine, Gertie." He squared his shoulders. "I'll make sure you have around the clock protection, if I have to do it myself."

"Well, that's sweet of you, but I've got Leroy. Marsha was staying with Dottie and that didn't help her none."

He glared at me. "Why haven't you figured this out yet?"

"Me?" What in the world? "You're the cop. Why don't we have any detectives assigned to help us out? Or the FBI?"

His shoulders sagged. "Because I didn't pass on the need."

Duane leaped to his feet like a bullet. "You had better not mean what I think you mean, you little twerp."

"I thought I could handle this." Bruce held up his hands to ward Duane off. "At first, I thought it was all just a prank. Then, when I realized it was something serious, it was too late."

"When did you figure that out?" I asked.

"When Dottie's brake line was cut."

Duane doubled up his fist, then obviously had second thoughts about striking a man in a police officer's uniform. "I don't know what to say." He moved back to his seat.

"Well, let's go over what we know." Bruce rubbed his hands together.

"Wait." Lindsey dashed to the drawer where I kept my clue-taking clipboard. "I'll write it all down."

"Somebody is filling out fake obits online. Nobody at the paper is verifying the information because they're short-staffed. I checked with Frank. See, I did do some detecting." He grinned, then frowned when Duane growled.

"The victims were all elderly women who lived alone. Also, we got back blood work from Little Rock." He eyed each of us. "I shouldn't be telling y'all this, but I desperately need your help. And, yes, I'll be contacting the feds. The blood work from each of the victims showed high doses of methamphetamine."

"Which, must have been slipped to them," I added. "None of the women were drug abusers, although Dottie enjoyed her wine."

"I think it best that all of you stay under one roof," Bruce suggested. "Duane, you too. The more people around, the less likely the killer will strike."

"Unless he blows all of us up in one big pow." Lindsey lifted her head from where she'd been taking notes. "At this point, whoever the bad guy is won't really care how many people he takes out. Grandma has a gas stove. Easy peasy…Boom!"

I cringed at her choice of words. The fact that she had a very good point caused my stomach to roil harder. "Leroy, turn off the pilot light to the gas."

"Already on it."

A glance at the clock showed I had thirty minutes to pick up Dottie. Fatigue weighted my limbs. My eyelids felt like sandpaper. Hopefully, I could pick her up, drop her off, and get home for a nap. After all, we had thirty days before danger struck. But, I didn't think I'd sleep well for any of it.

I pushed to my feet. "I've got to go pick up Dottie." Duane started to stand. "No, stay here and look after Mom and Lindsey, please. I'll be back within the hour." I bent over, gave him a kiss and headed back to the cottage to change my shoes and run a brush through my hair.

The drive to the hospital took longer than usual, most likely because my tiredness had me driving five miles under the speed limit. The parking lot was full when I pulled in, and the hands on my watch were pushing against twelve o'clock when I stepped up to the patient pick-up desk.

A man stood in front of me, arguing about release papers. My mind wandered, going over the notes Lindsey had written on her paper. Elderly. Alone. Drugs.

Oh, my. I knew who the killer was.

26

I texted the killer's identity to Duane and to Bruce, then shoved the phone back in my pocket. I needed to get Dottie home—fast. Careening into her hospital room, I came face-to-face with the exact person I texted about.

Darla Quincy clutched a pillow in her hands and leaned over Dottie. She smiled as I entered. "Is she going home today?" Darla made a great pretense of fluffing the pillow and putting it under Dottie's head. "My, that seems early."

"How'd you do it?"

"Do what?" A frown line appeared between her eyes. Why hadn't I noticed how deep it was before? "Do you have your column done for the paper?" Darla stepped toward me. "Or any advertisements sold? Frank is getting pretty temperamental about the state of his newspaper. As nosey as you are, you should have plenty of gossip for your column." She made a motion with her head to something over my shoulder.

How long would it take Duane or Bruce to get my message? Would they come here or go to her house? "I'm thinking about quitting my job at the paper. Are you the one in charge of the obituaries?"

"What am I not in charge of?"

Something jabbed me in the back. "Come on, Mrs. Steele. We're all going for a ride."

I sighed, recognizing Danny's voice. Of course the young man still tied to his mother's apron strings would also be involved. "Did y'all succeed in killing Dottie?"

"No." Darla spun me around. "You prevented that, thank you very much. Now, start walking and keep cool. If you alert anyone that everything isn't hunky dory, Danny will have to shoot you. After all, what better place to get shot than in a hospital? Take the stairwell, Danny. We don't want to bump into anyone in the elevator. Once we dispose of her, I'll come back and finish off the old woman."

My mind raced, trying to find a way out of the sticky situation. With Danny behind me, gun in hand, and Darla walking so close I could feel the gun in her pocket, escape seemed like a remote possibility.

Looking both ways, Darla pushed open the stairwell door. "It's a long walk to the bottom. Don't try anything, or you'll roll all the way, if you get my meaning."

Loud and clear. Another jab in the back sent me walking ahead of them. Instinct told me my only chance of surviving the day lay with Danny. Darla was nuttier than a chocolate peanut cluster.

Our footsteps echoed on the metal stairs encased in a concrete block corridor. I thought about screaming for help, but reconsidered. Doing so would result in one of two things: either I got a bullet in the back, or a shove down the stairs. Neither option sounded like fun.

"Why are you doing this?" I paused, one hand on the railing, and turned. "You could have walked out of Dottie's room and no one would have been the wiser."

Darla snorted. "I could tell by the look on your face when you saw me standing there, that you knew."

"No," I shook my head. "You were standing there with a pillow about to put it over her face."

"Semantics. Start walking." She pulled the gun from her pocket and turned her anger on her son. "Don't stand there like a baboon. Make her move."

"I've always liked her, Mom. She's done nothing to me. Why can't we let her go? We can head up to Canada or Mexico."

I doubted the other women had done anything to him either, but I wasn't going to argue. "Why did you pick the victims you did? I mean…none of them caused you any harm."

"I want people to pay attention." Darla shoved me.

I grabbed the railing with both hands. Vertigo attacked me as I glanced over the bars to the floor ten stories below.

"My mother died from a drug overdose and lay, undiscovered, in her apartment for a week! Do you know what it's like to hear that kind of news?"

Maybe she should've called her mother more. "These women weren't drug users."

"No, but they were alone. I gave people warning to see how many of these poor old women would still be alone after receiving a death threat." She shook her head, her gun hand trembling. Danny stood like a lump, head hanging, beside her. "They all were."

I moved down a few more steps, stalling for time. Where was Bruce?!

\"Hurry up!" Darla's screech bounced off the walls.

"I'm trying. It's difficult with a cast on."

"I'll shoot you in the other foot and leave you for dead, if you don't pick up the pace." Sweat beaded on her upper lip and plastered her bangs to her forehead. Darla was losing control, and I didn't want to be in front of her when her finger twitched.

If I could survive until we got outside, my chances of survival would double. As busy as St. Mary's hospital was, someone was bound to see us and be able to alert Bruce when he started asking questions.

Danny still shuffled along, head down, like a scolded child. Time to cut the apron strings boy, and do what was right. I tried to connect gazes with him, but he didn't even flinch when his mother screamed for me to hurry.

"Why don't y'all live together?" Keep 'em talking. It always worked in the movies.

"That is none of your business, nosey woman." Darla waved the gun. "If I tell you something like that, it'll wind up in the gossip column."

"Impossible if I'm dead." I took two more steps, holding tight to the rail. "Folks are saying the state took him away because you had a drug problem."

She paused. "Who said that?" She looked at Danny. "Have you been talking about us to people?"

"No, Mother. You told me not to." He stared up at her, the cold glare in his eyes more frightening than the gun in Darla's hand. "Don't I always do what you tell me?"

"Did she tell you to kill those women, Danny? Did she tell you to cut Dottie's brake line? Inject her with drugs?" I took another step. "I can't see your mother dirtying her hands. Not when she has you to do the dirty deed."

His mouth stretched into a thin line. "Mother killed Amber."

"Don't let her kill again." Another step. Far below I heard a door close. I increased my pace, the cast clumping against the metal stairs. "You can help me."

Darla laughed. "Stop playing mind games with him. I've trained him well. He only listens to me."

"I'm not a pet." He glared. "Stop treating me like one. I was going to be a father!"

"That girl wasn't worthy of you." She caressed his cheek.

These two had a sick perverted relationship. I took two more steps, trying my best not to make too much noise and divert their attentions back to me. A footstep scuffed below me. I prayed it was Bruce.

Duane would be nice, too, but his arrival would only put him in harm's way.

A door on the landing opened a crack. A nurse poked her head through. I shook my head and mouthed "Gun", right before diving through after her.

My shoulder connected with the doorframe. Shards of pain shot up my arm. It went limp.

I had no time to catch my breath. I struggled to my feet as Darla and Danny banged down the few stairs that separated us. Before the door opened again, I ducked into a closet and locked the door.

Holding my shoulder, I slid to the floor. They'd find me if I stayed there long enough, but I couldn't go on without rest. Tears sprang to my eyes as I rubbed what I guessed was a dislocated shoulder. How did I get myself in these fixes?

The floor I'd landed on didn't look like one occupied by patients. The hall had stretched long and lonely. Maybe a surgical ward? Even then, there were bound to be people. Someone would hear me cry for help.

"She's got to be close," Darla said from the other side of the door. "No one can move fast in a cast."

"Just leave her be and let's skip town." Danny sighed. "We can go to Mexico or Canada and start over."

"You've already said that. We can't go until all the loose ends are tied up."

Something thumped on the other side of the door.

"I still don't understand why you had me kill those women."

Oh, I should be recording this. I fumbled in my pocket for my phone, knocking over a broom. Freezing, I held my phone in my hand and held my breath.

"Did you hear that?" Darla lowered her voice. "I told you it was to teach people a lesson. Just because someone is old, doesn't mean they should be ignored."

"Still sounds like a stupid—"

My foot slipped, kicking over a pail. The clatter filled the small space.

A boom echoed, then the door flew open. Darla grabbed my good arm, hauling me to my feet. "You must be the stupidest person I've ever met. What's wrong with your arm?"

"I—"

Footsteps pounded from around the corner. Darla shoved me. "Get moving. We need you for leverage now. That stupid cop just arrived."

"Bruce!" I tried to hang back, but a knock on the back of the head with a gun got me moving again.

"Marsha." Duane raced down the hall, only to skid to a halt when he saw Darla and Danny's guns.

"Where do you think you can go?" Bruce asked. "Marsha is injured, the hospital is surrounded, and your son doesn't look happy to be here."

"Get it together, Danny." Darla held the gun to my head. "I've taught you to be tougher than this."

My legs threatened to give way. My gaze locked with Duane's. This was way worse than the car wreck in the last murder I'd gotten messed up in. That one took out the suspect. This one might be the end of me.

Keeping my eyes on Duane's pale face, I allowed the two killers to scoot me past my future husband and into the elevator. Once we made it to the parking lot, and past the one other cop that patrolled River Valley, Darla motioned for me to get into the passenger side of an older model Volvo.

"No." I stood as straight and rigid as possible. "You can shoot me right here. I am not getting into a car with you so you can dump my body in a vacant field somewhere. Either shoot me now, or leave me alone."

Danny set his gun on the roof of the car and stepped back. "I'm done. I've been your puppet for too long, Mother. I won't be a part of any more killing. He put his hands on top of his head and walked back toward the hospital.

I grinned. "Now what, Darla? You've allowed the guilt over your mother's death to poison every relationship you've ever had. Maybe you can actually form a nice one in prison. I've heard there are a lot of lonely people behind bars."

"Shut up." She chewed her bottom lip. "I'm trying to think."

While she did, I shuffled sideways in an attempt to get closer to Danny's gun. Darla seemed riveted on the view of her son being handcuffed. At least I hoped so. *God, don't let me fail.*

"Look what you've done to Danny. Poor misguided boy. He only loved you so much he killed for you. Now what? Are you going to allow him to watch you get shot?" Almost there. "At least he came to his senses."

"Shut up." She never looked back.

I grabbed the gun with my good hand, lunged forward, conked her on the back of the head, and slid down the car to the hard pavement. Seconds later, I found myself wrapped in Duane's arms, while paramedics raced to our side.

Darla stirred when Bruce twisted her hands behind her back. "Want me to taze her, Marsha?"

"Tempting, but no. If I felt better, I'd taze her myself."

Duane helped me to my feet, taking care of my shoulder. Every jar sent flames of fire down my arm.

"Duane?"

"Yes, my love." He lifted me as if I weighed no more than a child.

I rested my head on his shoulder. "How does June tenth sound for a wedding?"

"That's our one year anniversary. It sounds perfect."

"Then kiss me."

He lowered his head and helped me forget about the pain.

THE END

ABOUT THE AUTHOR

www.cynthiahickey.com
Cynthia Hickey is a multi-published and best-selling author of cozy mysteries and romantic suspense. She has taught writing at many conferences and small writing retreats. She and her husband run the publishing press, Winged Publications. They live in Arizona and Arkansas, becoming snowbirds with three dogs. They have ten grandchildren who keep them busy and tell everyone they know that "Nana is a writer."

www.ingramcontent.com/pod-product-compliance
Lightning Source LLC
Chambersburg PA
CBHW061033120726
47910CB00006B/2236